A LEGAL FICTI

'I must hurry and tell you what's happened now, or this call will cost you a fortune. I'm staying in Oldersfield at the moment, looking after Mother's teashop for her, while she's in Spain. And yesterday in a saleroom here I saw the Decayed Gentlewoman ... No, wait a minute!' she said as Colin started to speak. 'I swear it's the same picture, Colin. It's in a different frame, and perhaps it's even a bit more battered than I remembered, and I can't think of any reason for its turning up here after getting stolen in the Highlands, but here it is, all the same. And my first thought was I ought to go to the police about it. Then I thought, why worry about that, when it would only lead to a lot of fuss and bother and she can't be worth that much, anyway? She isn't, is she, Colin? It was your car those men were after, not what was inside it.'

**Also by the same author,
and available in Coronet Crime:**

Alive and Dead
A Foot in the Grave
Murder Among Friends

Praise for Elizabeth Ferrars:

'(She) has had a long distinguished career as a
first-class writer of detective stories . . . intellec-
tually at a higher level than most contemporary
writing. The same is true of her literary cultiv-
ation. They are, in the best sense, sophisticated'
C. P. Snow

'A name I read for pleasure, not just business'
Antony Price in The Scotsman

'Her style: acute observation of character, racy
dialogue and a particularly ingenious solution'
Guernsey Evening Press and Star

'Civilised and entertaining, at times thought-
provoking'
Melvyn Barnes in Murder in Print

A Legal Fiction

Elizabeth Ferrars

CORONET BOOKS
Hodder and Stoughton

A CIP catalogue record for this title is available from the British Library

ISBN 0-340-54408-2

Printed and bound in Great Britain for Hodder and Stoughton Paperbacks, a division of Hodder and Stoughton Ltd., Mill Road, Dunton Green, Sevenoaks, Kent TN13 2YA (Editorial) Office: 47 Bedford Square, London WC1B 3DP) by Clays Ltd., St Ives plc.

ACKNOWLEDGMENTS

I wish to express my gratitude to Professor T. B. Smith, Sheriff J. G. Wilson and Mr. David Baxandall for the help they have given me with this story, and at the same time to affirm that any blunders in it are not the responsibility of these experts, but wholly my own.

E.F.

CHAPTER ONE

As THE TRAIN from Edinburgh crept into King's Cross, the station loudspeaker was making one of its baffling announcements, the words of which, as usual, were swallowed up in echoes ringing round the great, grimy roof. Colin Lockie, coming bleary-eyed out of his second-class sleeper, paid no attention to the unintelligible voice. Wearing a grey tweed overcoat and carrying his briefcase, the only luggage he had brought with him, he edged his way along the corridor of the train and stepped out on to the platform. He was thinking of the bath and the breakfast that he was going to have in the station hotel. The very large breakfast, far larger than he ever thought of cooking for himself. He would have fruit-juice, porridge, sausages and bacon, a lot of toast. Or should he have kippers instead of sausages?

His mind was hovering between these alternatives when the loudspeaker spoke again. This time it sounded shockingly clear.

"Will Dr. Colin Lockie please go at once to the station master's office?"

Colin's first startled thought was that it was a mistake. Then that this had been bound to happen sometime. It could not always be others to whom calamity happened. Sooner or later fate would knock at one's own door. But it puzzled him who could have known that he would be on that train. And to whom was he so important that they would go to the trouble of having him summoned in that voice of doom? Feeling a little cold as he ran over the names of his nearest and dearest, he found that none of them seemed somehow quite near or dear enough to have faced the ordeal of coping with British Railways in its early morning torpor merely to reach him. So perhaps, after all, he had not heard the voice correctly. Perhaps it had not been his name that had been called.

The voice immediately repeated it distinctly. "Will Dr. Colin Lockie please go at once to the station master's office?"

It jerked him into action. He strode swiftly to the barrier. But there the press of people prevented him from moving on any faster than anyone else and he had time to make up his mind that although he was probably about to receive some very serious shock, he would behave calmly. He would walk on, would ask a porter where the station master's office was, would present himself there, take the blow, whatever it was, without change of expression, say a courteous, "Thank you," to the unfortunate official whose duty it had been to deal the blow, remove himself as fast as possible, and then . . .

A vision of sausages and kippers swam before his eyes.

The truth was, Colin was fiendishly hungry. He was a big young man with wide shoulders, powerful muscles and a very active brain, and whatever his emotional state might be, his considerable strength took a good deal of keeping up.

Finding his way to the station master's office without having to ask where it was, he went in and said to a young man behind a counter, who was sleepily polishing his spectacles, "I'm Colin Lockie."

There was a pause. The clerk breathed on his spectacles and gave them another rub with his handkerchief.

"Yes?" he said at last.

"There was a message for me on the loudspeaker," Colin said. "It told me to come here."

"Oh." The clerk tried to smother a yawn. "Well, what did you say your name was?"

"Colin Lockie."

"Lockie. All right." The yawn escaped. "I'll see."

He turned and wandered away.

He was gone for less, probably, than half a minute. But it was a half minute during which Colin's dread of what he was to hear had had time to mount to such a painful pitch that by the time the sleepy clerk returned, he hated him with all the force of his pounding heart.

The man was reading what was written on a slip of paper.

"Doctor Colin Lockie?" he asked.

"Yes."

"Well, will you telephone Miss Winter, Oldersfield 2571, immediately?"

It meant nothing to Colin. He knew no Miss Winter. He did not know Oldersfield or anyone who lived there. He did not even know where Oldersfield was.

"There's been a mistake," he said. "That can't be the message for me."

"Oh," the clerk said and turned the slip of paper over as if there might be something written on the back. Finding it blank, he turned it again and read it through slowly to himself. "Well," he said at last, "it says it's for Dr. Colin Lockie."

Holding himself in with an effort, Colin said, "Would you mind checking with whoever took the message? I think it must have got mixed up with another one."

"Oh," the clerk said. "Well, all right."

He wandered away again.

When he returned, he brought with him an elderly man with a cold, wideawake stare which fastened on Colin's face like a bitter draught.

"Good morning, doctor, there's been no mistake, I can assure you," he said. "I spoke to the lady myself. She convinced me the matter was of the greatest urgency, or I may say I should not have agreed to having the message given out over our loudspeaker system. We don't make a habit of giving out trivial messages, as you're no doubt aware, sir. She said it concerned an accident——"

"Oh, but," Colin interrupted, "I'm not that sort of doctor."

This had happened to him before. His landlady, for instance, misled by the way that Colin's letters were addressed, was still unconvinced that the title doctor, conferred on him five years ago by London University for his work on the development of vascular bundles in leaves, did not qualify him to treat her varicose veins.

The second clerk had taken no notice of the interruption. "An accident, she said, at a place called Ard-something-or-other, in Scotland. She said the occupant of the car, who had disappeared and was thought to be suffering from loss of memory, had reappeared in Oldersfield and that you were urgently required there for identification purposes. That was the full message, sir. There's been no mistake."

Colin stared. Normally his mind worked fairly fast and, except about such matters as what day of the week it was, or where he had left his car-keys, or how much money he had in the bank, it was not easy to confuse him. But he had not slept much on the train and now sense and nonsense overlapped so absurdly in the clerk's statement that he felt as if he were on the edge of a dream.

That accident at Ardachoil, if you could call it an accident, had happened two and a half years ago. And he had been the only passenger in the car. And he had recovered his memory quite fully as soon as he had recovered consciousness.

But at least it seemed that the message was meant for him.

"I see," he said. "Thanks. By the way, where's Oldersfield?"

In Kent, they told him. Still bewildered, Colin took the slip of paper with Miss Winter's name and telephone number on it and left the office.

She had asked him to ring her up immediately, and that meant, he supposed, before he had even had his bath or breakfast, which was a pity. Still, it would be an easier thing to do from a quiet call-box inside the hotel than in the noise of the station. Walking out into the station yard and the raw chill of the spring morning, he crossed to the hotel entrance, went in, made sure that he had enough change in his pockets to make the call, and went to a telephone.

As soon as the connection was made, he heard the receiver at the other end lifted. A woman's voice said swiftly, " Oldersfield 2571."

It was so quick that she must have been waiting beside the telephone.

" Miss Winter? I'm Colin Lockie," he said. " You left a message——"

" Colin! " Her voice sounded young, excited and quite unfamiliar. " Colin, how wonderful that I've managed to get hold of you at last! I've been telephoning everywhere ever since yesterday afternoon and only been told you weren't there. And so I thought I was going to have to act entirely on my own responsibility. You see, the sale starts at nine o'clock and she's in Lot Seven, in among all the junk, so they'll get there in no time at all. So I've got to know if you want me to go ahead and how high I can go."

" Please forgive me," Colin said cautiously, " but I don't think I know what you're talking about."

" But you got my message. Didn't you understand it? I made it as clear as I dared, without actually giving away that it wasn't a matter of life and death. If they'd realised that, I thought, they mightn't have given it out at all. So that's why I put in the bit about the passenger who vanished from your car when those men knocked you out on the road from Ardachoil."

" There wasn't any passenger," Colin said.

" There was the Decayed Gentlewoman, wasn't there? Don't you remember how we used to call her the Decayed Gentlewoman, Colin? "

As she spoke that preposterous name, which he had probably not heard since he was a boy of fourteen or thereabouts, Colin's mind seemed to go completely blank for a moment. Then all kinds of things came tumbling back into it.

" Good God above," he said softly, " you're Ginny Jerrold."

There was a silence, then in a different and older-sounding voice, she said, " You mean you didn't know you were speaking to me?"

" How could I? " he said. " I was told to ring up a Miss Winter. I never knew any Miss Winter."

" You mean you never heard . . ." She let the sentence fade, sounding sad that he knew so little.

" Then it should have been Mrs. Winter," he said. " You're married."

" No. My mother married. I took my stepfather's name. Years and years ago. Did you really hear nothing about it? "

" I'm afraid I didn't, Ginny."

" Not even whispered rather surreptitiously, when you weren't supposed to hear? "

" Well, perhaps . . ."

" No, you didn't. I understand. Once those awful aunts of yours caught on about poor Mother, our names weren't mentioned."

" I never actually knew what happened," Colin said, " except that you stopped coming."

That was true. He had never understood what had happened to Ginny and her attractive, widowed mother. For a time they had been welcome guests at Ardachoil, then they had disappeared and apparently been easily forgotten by the three aunts who had provided Colin with a home during school holidays, while his parents—his father had been in the Colonial Service—travelled the earth.

Yet the aunts normally cherished friendship. They were so loyal to every memory of it that they still sent Christmas cards to people whom they had not seen for thirty years. So the way that they had allowed Mrs. Jerrold and her daughter to vanish out of their lives had clearly required some explaining.

"Well, it doesn't matter," Ginny Winter said. "I must hurry and tell you what's happened now, or this call will cost you a fortune. I'm staying in Oldersfield at the moment, looking after Mother's teashop for her, while she's in Spain. And yesterday in a saleroom here I saw the Decayed Gentlewoman . . . No, wait a minute!" she added swiftly, as Colin started to speak. "I swear it's the same picture, Colin. It's in a different frame, and perhaps it's even a bit more battered than I remembered, and I can't think of any reason for its turning up here after getting stolen in the Highlands, but here it is, all the same. And my first thought was I ought to go to the police about it. Then I thought, why worry about that, when it would only lead to a lot of fuss and bother and she can't be worth much, anyway? She isn't, is she, Colin? It was your car those men were after, not what was inside it."

"Oh yes, the police decided they were two men who'd escaped from Barlinnie and wanted a car for a getaway," said Colin. "But, listen, Ginny. This doesn't really make sense. Don't you think you've just turned up another copy of the same picture, whatever it is?"

"No," she said. "I'm absolutely certain it's our Decayed Gentlewoman. I can't explain why I'm so certain, any more than I could explain why—well, why I'd probably be certain it was you, if I suddenly saw you. Unless, of course, you've changed an awful lot. Have you changed an awful lot, Colin? You were a very large, very fat boy, with very pink cheeks."

"Was I? Then I haven't changed much, I suppose," he said. "What I mainly remember about you is your imagination."

God, yes, he thought, Ginny's imagination!

"I'm not imagining anything now," she said. "I recognised her instantly, as I would an old friend. And the question is, do you want me to do anything about it? Shall I bid for her and see if I can get her back for your horrible aunts?"

"If you're sure . . ."

"I *am* sure."

"Then—yes, please, Ginny. I know they'd love to have her back."

"I warn you," she told him, " you'll have to buy two or three even more awful pictures along with her, and a cracked mirror and two sets of brass fire-irons and a rusty electric iron."

"All in Lot Seven?"

"Yes. But I shouldn't think the price for a collection like that could possibly go high, would you?"

"Do you think ten pounds would cover it?"

"Ten pounds?" Her voice shot up. "It'll *never* go as high as that!"

"Well, I could afford ten pounds. And thank you for all the trouble you're taking."

"That's all right, then. Now tell me," she said, "where can I get in touch with you to let you know what happens?"

"My Edinburgh address——"

"I know your Edinburgh address. I meant to-day. I

suppose——" She hesitated. "I suppose you couldn't come down here yourself, Colin. When I heard you were going to be in London, I rather hoped you might be able to. I know you can't get here in time for the sale, but it might be a good idea to come, all the same. I mean, if you don't feel quite sure it's the same picture when you see it, we could probably get Joe Lake—it's in his sale-room—to take it back and offer it again. He's a friend of my mother's and I'm sure he'd do it for us. On the other hand, if it *is* the same picture, he might be able to tell you something about how he got hold of it."

"I'm awfully sorry," Colin said, "I can't manage to-day. There's something I've got to do . . ." With a slight shock the thought of what he had come to London to do came back to him. "It's something I can't put off. And I'm going home again to-night."

"Oh dear, that's a pity, when you're actually so near for once."

"But I could ring you up again later to-day."

"Will you do that then?"

"What time?"

"Any time."

"All right. And . . . Wait a minute!" He thought she was going to ring off and suddenly he knew that he did not want to leave the matter there. "Ginny, if it's important, I haven't absolutely got to go back to Edinburgh to-night. Perhaps I could come down to Oldersfield to-morrow."

"Well, we'll talk about that when you ring up," she said. "Good-bye."

"No, hold on! Tell me, Ginny, how did you ever hear about the car business and the picture disappearing?"

But now the dialling tone was buzzing impatiently at his ear.

He had an impulse to ring her up again at once and

repeat his question. He wanted to know how she knew so much about him. The attack on him and the theft of the car had been reported in the local press, but he was fairly sure that there had been no mention of the loss of the picture. But when he felt in his pocket for more change, he found that he had not enough for another call to Oldersfield. Giving up the idea of ringing Ginny up again just then, he emerged from the call-box and went to have his bath and breakfast.

CHAPTER TWO

IT WAS AN INVITATION to read a paper to the Royal Society that had brought Colin to London that day. The paper was on differentiation in the apex of the shoot. He was not usually nervous when he had to talk about his work, but this was the first time that he had been invited to one of the Thursday afternoon meetings at Burlington House and there was a moment, as the President started to introduce him, when the portrait on the wall of Charles II seemed to leer with deadly humour straight at Colin, as if asking him what he thought he was doing there among all these learned men. He felt that he would never be able to justify his presence.

But once he was on his feet, things felt better. For the first few minutes his hands seemed to possess a disconcerting life of their own, quite unconnected with the rest of him, weaving mad, meaningless patterns in the air around him. But at some point, perhaps when he realised that he was at least holding the attention of his hearers, they grew quiet, and when it was over and he again met the knowing, dissipated gaze of the founder of the Society, it only acted as a reminder that he was to ring Ginny up to find out what had happened about that other portrait.

The Decayed Gentlewoman . . .

As he walked out into Piccadilly, he smiled at the memory. It had been Ginny who had thought of that name for the picture. Almost everything in her world in those days had possessed a private human identity and so naturally had needed a name. And all the other pictures at Ardachoil had had names of their own already. There had been the Laughing Cavalier, the Blue Boy, the Birth of Venus. So it had seemed only fair that the picture of the sad-looking lady, which had hung in a corner of the dining-room, where the end of the sideboard had cast a perpetual shadow across it, should have a name too.

Colin remembered that he had found the one invented by Ginny exquisitely funny. For a time both the children had been in love with the sparkling humour of it and had dragged the phrase somehow into almost everything they said, until the aunts, maddened, had tried to put a ban on it. They couldn't, they had said, see anything in the least funny about it. Moreover, it wasn't really very nice. Of course, that had only made the children laugh more uproariously than ever.

Colin was meaning to go to the Underground station to ring Ginny up, but as he walked along he found Peter Schleier at his elbow, and, at Schleier's suggestion, they went to the Earl Grey for a drink, then to a steak house in Leicester Square for dinner.

Colin had known Schleier since his Imperial College days. Schleier had been a lecturer there when Colin had come from Glasgow University to do a Ph.D. in London. Later Schleier had gone to Australia for some years, returning recently to become head of the department of biology at the new University of Crewe. He was a short, dark, dogmatic man who had come from Berlin with his parents just before the war, as a child of fifteen, and had never lost the accent that he had had then, although his vocabulary had rapidly become many times more extensive than any normal Englishman's.

He set out now to praise Colin's recent research in heart-warming polysyllables. It gave Colin a cheering glow inside and along with the beer and a thick, tender steak, rounded off the day so agreeably that it was past nine o'clock when he again remembered that he was supposed to call Ginny. Hurrying the rest of the meal, he said good-bye to Schleier and went to the telephones in Leicester Square.

When he heard Ginny Winter speak, he began an apology for having left the call so late.

"Oh, it doesn't matter," she answered. There was a listlessness in her voice that had not been there before. "It wouldn't have made any difference."

"Why, has something gone wrong?" he asked.

"I'm afraid so," she said.

"What is it?" He thought it was probably that she was offended with him for not having rung up sooner.

"I didn't think you'd want to pay a hundred and ten pounds for the picture, so I stopped bidding and we lost it. I'm terribly sorry."

"Oh well, that's nothing to worry about. The aunts needn't even know——" He stopped abruptly. The meaning of what she had said sank in. "*A hundred and ten pounds!*"

"Yes," she said.

"For that picture—for our poor old Decayed Gentlewoman? It went for a hundred and ten pounds?"

"Yes—unless it was one of the other things in the lot. But really they all looked far worse than she did."

"And you went on bidding . . .?" The thought of what he had just escaped made sweat break out on Colin's forehead.

"Yes, I went on up to a hundred pounds, because I thought it must be worth the money if someone else wanted it so badly," she said. "But at a hundred pounds I got cold feet."

"Thank God for that!" said Colin. "Who bought it?"

"Oh, I don't know. A man with a horrid, pale green face and a nasty voice. I hated him."

"Perhaps he was just trying to push you up for the owner and misjudged things."

"Do you think so? I could ask Joe Lake about that. He's the auctioneer—I told you that, didn't I? He looked very surprised at my bidding and made awful faces to stop me, but I got carried away. It's a wonderful feeling while it lasts, but it's terrible afterwards. A complete anti-climax. Almost a feeling there's nothing left to live for."

"On the other hand . . ." Colin said thoughtfully.

"Yes?"

He frowned out at the lights of Leicester Square, the dense stream of traffic, the glare of neon on a cinema. He was remembering the day when he had set out to take the picture to Edinburgh for cleaning. Just south of the point where the little road that ran along the edge of the loch to Ardachoil joined the main road south to Lochgilphead, a man, apparently hurt, had been lying across the middle of the road. Colin had stopped his car and got out to see what was wrong and was bending over him when something had come down on the back of his head. He had had to spend a week in hospital with concussion.

"Yes?" Ginny said again after a moment.

"I was just saying to myself," Colin said, "suppose that picture *is* worth a hundred and ten pounds. Perhaps even more."

"Oh, that's an awful thought," she said, "because he's got it—the man with the nasty voice. It's gone. I lost it."

"Actually, no, because it happens to be stolen property," said Colin. "If it's the same picture, it still belongs to my aunts, whoever's bought it since it was taken. At least,

I think that's the law. And if it's even moderately valuable and not just the junk we thought it was, it might be worth some fuss and bother with the police to get it back. Have you thought of asking your auctioneer friend where he got it?"

"Oh yes, and he said something about the estate of an old woman down here who died a few weeks ago. They were mostly her things Joe was selling to-day."

Colin was silent again, trying to make up his mind about several things all at the same time and to foresee what he might be getting himself into if he did what he suddenly had a very strong inclination to do.

"You know, I think I'd better come to Oldersfield to-morrow," he said.

A little to his surprise, because he had somehow assumed that Ginny would jump at the suggestion, she did not answer at once. Then she said hesitantly, "Yes, that might be best. But the picture isn't here any more, you know. The man took it away with him."

"Have you got his address?"

"No," she said.

"Couldn't you get it from your friend Joe?"

"I suppose I could."

"I'll come down in the morning then. Where do I find you?"

"At the Green Tree Café. It's in the market place. It's quite near the station. You won't need a taxi. But, Colin——"

"Yes?"

"No, it doesn't matter. It can keep till to-morrow. Good-night."

"Good-night," he said.

Picking up his briefcase, he left the call-box and instead of going to King's Cross, walked towards Bloomsbury to find a hotel.

Next morning he took a train from Charing Cross to Oldersfield, which deposited him there at a quarter to twelve. It took only a few minutes to find the market place, which he reached by walking along an alley between half-timbered cottages, which branched out of the narrow, impossibly congested main street. It was a street of seventeenth and eighteenth century houses. Almost everything in Oldersfield, he found, was old, except for its traffic problem.

The market itself looked as if it had probably been carried on in the same place for hundreds of years. The stalls of flowers, vegetables, haberdashery, cheap jewellery, cakes, sweets and second-hand china, looked as established on the uneven cobbles of the square as the wavy-roofed old houses were around it.

Some of these houses had had shop-windows cut out of their rosy brick or plastered fronts. Some had the brass plates of solicitors or house-agents by their doors. From one of them, a corner building, a faded awning projected over the pavement, covering a jumble of secondhand furniture. Written up on the side of this house were the words, "Lake's Saleroom." About three doors away from it was the Green Tree Café. It had a wooden sign hanging over its door, a cut-out of a tree that might have been anything from an oak to a Christmas tree, but at least was green, very green indeed. Colin made his way towards it.

The café had one fair-sized window overlooking the market place. Across the window were two glass shelves, on which plates of scones, sponge sandwiches, fruit-cake and shortbread biscuits were set out. They had a not very homemade and infinitely tired air. A menu-card, stuck to the inside of the window with pieces of transparent tape, announced that lunch, consisting of cream of tomato soup, steak pie and two veg. and bread and butter pudding or sherry trifle, would be served from twelve till two o'clock.

The card was spotty and looked faded by exposure.

Inside, Colin could see an old man sitting at a plastic-topped table with a cup of tea in front of him. He had bent shoulders and a lined face with blankly dreaming eyes. He looked as if he might have been sitting there over the same cup of tea for the last hour. A stout young woman in a mackintosh and headscarf sat at another table. She had a three-year-old child with her, whom she was feeding with teaspoonfuls of chocolate éclair. Her own lunch seemed to consist of tea and a bun. Someone whom Colin could not quite see was moving about behind a tea-urn on a counter. It might, he supposed, be Ginny.

Suddenly Colin found himself remembering with extra-ordinary clarity the child that Ginny had been.

She had had an exciting and curiously deliberate brand of recklessness, an inventive mind, a rather sarcastic turn of speech and moods of loving dependence on him which generally followed tantrums that had occurred when she had had a little too much crime on her conscience. She had been shy mannered, bright haired and feather-light in her movements. Colin had loved her, protected her and some-times feared her.

And here she was now, running this awful café.

His hand dropped from the door. He turned away and walked off slowly across the market place.

He stopped when he came to a flower stall and bought a bunch of jonquils. The gesture helped to take his mind off the stale cakes and the spotty menu. Besides, the least he could do, he thought, on arriving like this, after fifteen years, to visit the first love of his life, was to come bearing flowers. Grasping the jonquils, he returned to the café, pushed the door open and went in.

He saw then that the woman behind the counter was not Ginny. She was at least seventy, had a hare-lip, a large pale, placid face and grey hair. When she started to ask him what she could do for him, she spoke with a strong local accent.

But the tinkle of the bell on the street door brought another woman darting out of a door at the far end of the room, and although she had grown rather taller than Colin had for some reason expected and was wearing an overall of apple-green nylon, an anonymous sort of garment that might have robbed anyone of identity, he had no difficulty in recognising her. Her fair hair, cropped so short that it looked like a thick sort of golden fur growing on her small, delicately shaped head, her high, slightly bulging forehead, her long-lashed grey eyes, her thin cheeks were all more unchanged than he would have thought possible.

In a way, it was disturbing that she was so unchanged. It made her look more like an elongated version of the child that she had once been than a young woman who had had fifteen years in which to do some growing up.

She gave a soft exclamation of surprise when she saw him. It might have been at the jonquils, or at his size, or even at his being there at all. Taking the flowers from him, she made a slightly exaggerated show of pleasure over them.

" Just like the ones at Ardachoil," she said with a somewhat artificial little sigh. " They'd gone wild all up the hillside at the back, hadn't they? Wonderful Ardachoil! Come in and tell me all about it."

In fact the flowers that had gone wild on the hillside behind the house, after having been very carefully naturalised there by the aunts, were daffodils. Ginny's memory of the place was apparently not very clear.

Following her through the café into the kitchen from which she had just emerged, Colin saw a woman, almost as old as the one behind the counter, working at the stove.

Ginny told her to call her if she was needed, and led the way across the kitchen and down some stone steps into the basement. She took Colin into a big room, furnished as a bed-sitting-room and badly lit by two barred windows at pavement level.

Switching on the light and an electric fire that stood in the old fireplace, she asked, "Have you had any lunch yet? If not, we could have some bread and cheese here, or go out and have it somewhere decent. I'm not trying to manœuvre you into taking me out for an expensive lunch. I'd prefer the bread and cheese. But just in case you require more solid food, I'm telling you the alternatives."

"What about the tomato soup and the steak pie and two veg.?" Colin asked.

"Oh, that—it's off. Been off ever since Mother went away. I keep forgetting to take the card down. Or perhaps I leave it up on purpose, because of the sense of power it gives me, being able to say, 'It's off.' You can see the shock of it go right through people."

"Then what do you give them to eat in this place?"

"Sandwiches and buns and ice-cream and beans on toast, when the Heavens sisters are feeling up to it. By the way, their name really is Heavens. I didn't make it up. One couldn't make up a name like that."

"Well, if you can be spared, wouldn't it be a good idea to go out to a place where we can have a drink and a square meal?" Colin suggested. "I'm quite hungry."

She gave him a sweet, brief smile. "I remember you always were. But I'll have to put these flowers in water first." She picked up a plain black pot from the top of a bookcase, turned it upside down, at which three buttons and a safety-pin fell out on the floor, and went to the door. She paused then and spoke with sudden intensity. "Colin, it was lovely to be given them! And I'm very glad you came, because I've a lot of things to tell you. I shan't be long."

She disappeared into some other shadowy part of the basement.

Waiting for her, thinking that she was taking longer than necessary to put the flowers in water, Colin supposed that she must be smartening herself up to go out. However, when she reappeared presently, she was still in her green overall. She was carrying a tray with some bread, butter and cheese on it, as well as the jonquils arranged in the black pot.

She put the tray down on the table in the middle of the room.

"I thought after all it would be better to eat here," she said. "Don't you think so really? It'll be easier to talk. And I can manage the drinks all right. Mother generally has some of most things." She opened a corner cupboard and revealed rows of bottles. "What would you like— sherry, gin, vodka, whisky?"

Colin dropped into a chair. An odd sense of familiarity had suddenly gripped him. He had the feeling that he had been here before. Ginny had so often played the same trick on him. She had let him have the illusion that she was ready to do whatever he preferred, go out, stay at home, play cowboys, play chess, then she had done what she intended all along. Or, at least, done what she had discovered that she wanted to do as soon as he revealed that he wanted to do something different.

"Beer, please," he said.

She poured out beer for him and sherry for herself, then sat down facing him across the table.

"Ginny, I don't get any of this!" he exclaimed. "What are you doing here? What's your mother doing here?"

"I told you, Mother isn't here," she said. "She's in

Spain on a bus tour. She's one of the queer people who
like bus tours. She likes being pushed around among a lot
of other people and being told what to do next."

" I meant, what are you trying to do with this place? "
Colin asked. " What's been happening to you both? "

" That it's come to this? " She laughed. " Mother calls
it a teashop, because she thinks it has a refined, pre-war sort
of sound, but of course it's just a caff and always will be."

" What made her start it? "

" Well, she was at a loose end and Joe Lake persuaded
her it would be a sure-fire thing if she did the right things
with it."

" Joe Lake seems to be quite an influence in your life."

" In a way," she agreed. " He worries about Mother and
wants to put her on her feet. He doesn't realise she hasn't
really got feet to stand on."

" Presumably then she hasn't done the right things."

She met his eyes for a moment and Colin realised suddenly that there was nothing youthful in them. It was as if
something behind them had aged so fast that the immature
shell of her body had had no chance to keep up.

" She didn't start very well," she said. " There was the
problem of the Heavens sisters, for instance. Mother took
them over with the rest of the fittings, and said it would
be a shame to push them out, as they were so old. But they
were more than a little set in their ways and always discouraged all Mother's bright ideas. And Mother dis-
courages very easily when it comes to a job of work."

" And where do you fit into it all? "

" At the moment I'm just making use of some free board
and lodging and keeping an eye on things and doing a few
odds and ends of decorating. I've done this room, for
instance, and re-painted the sign over the door. Did you
notice it? "

"Yes, very handsome," Colin said. "Are you a painter?"

"Of course not. But at least it's green now and catches the eye."

"What do you do when you aren't here?" he asked.

"Oh—various things." Her gaze moved away from his and attached itself to a corner of the ceiling. "This and that. I'm really just like Mother—I drift from one thing to another—except that I'll never be as sweet as she is. There's something very sour in my nature. Now let me tell you about how I saw that picture——"

"Tell me something else first," Colin interrupted. "Tell me why you and your mother stopped coming to Ardachoil."

"We stopped being asked, that was all," she said.

"But why?"

"Ask your aunts."

"No, Ginny, tell me."

She gave a shrug of her shoulders and looked at him again, her big grey eyes sardonic.

"I suppose your aunts found out that Mother wasn't a widow at all. You see, when Mother and your Aunt Dolly made friends during the war, when they were both in the A.T.S., Mother was making herself out to be a widow. Naturally, since she had me to explain. I don't imagine anyone but your Aunt Dolly believed her for a moment. But Aunt Dolly apparently did, and she was so sorry for us both and realised I was about the same age as that little boy whom she and her sisters had to look after in the holidays, and that I'd make such a nice companion for him. Which, let me say, I did my best to be, even if you don't remember it. But Mother must have let the cat out of the bag somehow and so the invitations stopped."

"And then?"

"*And then!*" she said, suddenly fierce. "Is this some

sort of examination? What happened then, or a bit later, was that Mother married Harry Winter, who was a traveller in electrical gadgets and a darling, but he was dying already of lung cancer, so she only got a genuine widowhood out of it—apart from his life's savings, which may have been what she really married him for. I don't know about that. I just know what happened and that he was a darling."

Colin reached for the loaf of bread and began to cut it.

"You're quite right, something in your nature has got a bit soured," he said. "I don't understand about my aunts. They aren't usually so narrow-minded."

"Aren't they?" she said. "They used always to make me feel I spent my time stumbling from one deadly sin to the next. Yet I was really a very quiet, harmless child."

"Is that what you think?" She might, he considered, have given the aunts some credit for being as good to her as they had been at first, whatever had happened later. "About the picture . . ."

"Yes," she said quickly, as if she were relieved that he was at last ready to talk about it. "Well?"

"I don't understand how you knew it had been stolen."

"I think I must have read it in the papers," she said.

"I don't think it got into the papers."

"Oh, it did. I'm sure it did. I can remember Mother reading it out to me and saying, "That must be that fat little boy you used to play with at Ardachoil—d'you remember him, Ginny?" She took a slice of bread and began to butter it. "You aren't so fat now, but you're fairly enormous."

"I don't believe I ever was fat," he said, smiling. "It was sheer bone and muscle. And, you see, there never was anything in the papers about the picture disappearing."

"I'm sure there was."

"Not about the picture. Only about the hold-up and the car. Nothing was said about the picture—any more than about my suitcase and my Thermos and sandwiches. Nobody thought it was important."

"But now you think perhaps it was?"

"I don't know. I don't know yet if it's really the same picture. But I do know there was nothing about it in the papers."

"I tell you there was. I remember Mother reading it out. Or anyway . . ." She wrinkled her forehead uncertainly. "I remember her telling me about it. It doesn't matter, does it? I know I heard about it somehow and as soon as I saw it in Joe's saleroom on Wednesday afternoon—we shut on Wednesday afternoons, so I was prowling around, seeing if I could perhaps pick up some nicer sort of plates to go in the window upstairs. Actually it's the cakes that need changing, more than the plates, but the Heavens sisters mightn't like that . . . Well, as I was saying, I was poking around and suddenly I saw the picture. I knew it at once and I remembered about its being stolen. So in spite of the fact that my feeling for your aunts borders on the indifferent, I thought I really ought to try to get in touch with you, in case you'd like me to get it back. A pure piece of sentiment. Old times, and so on. And, as you know, I thought I'd get it easily for a few pounds and it was the shock of my life when someone else started bidding for it."

"How did you know how to get in touch with me?"

She dropped her piece of bread and cheese on to her plate and pushed her chair back sharply from the table. Its feet made a screeching sound on the stone floor.

"Is this what you're always like, Colin? How many more questions are you going to ask me? Because I think I've had nearly enough of them. I happened to know you were a lecturer at Edinburgh University because—because a friend of mine went to a job there a couple of years ago and one day he happened to mention you."

" Who is he? " Colin asked.

" His name's John Clitheroe. He's in History, I think, or perhaps it's Economics. Something like that. Well, so of course I rang up the university on Wednesday, and somebody told me to try another number, and somebody there told me to try another, and so on, until at last I got on to a nice man who said his name was Fordyce, and he knew you were going to London that night and he said he'd see if your landlady knew which train you were going on, and then he'd ring me back. Which he did."

" Forsythe," Colin said. " Bob Forsythe."

Bob Forsythe was a research student whose work Colin had been directing for the last year. But John Clitheroe was a name that meant nothing to him.

Restraining the urge to ask further questions about him, he said, " It sounds as though you had an expensive afternoon, with all that telephoning."

" Never mind." She hitched her chair back to the table and picked up her bread and cheese. " I'll make some coffee in a moment," she said, " then we'll go and see the Lakes. But there's no hurry, because they won't get back from the pub for some time. They always have a pretty long, pretty alcoholic lunch-hour."

" Does ' they ' mean Lake and his wife? " Colin asked.

" Yes, Joe and Beryl. But before we go round there's something I want to tell you about them." She put her head a little on one side, looking into Colin's face with a certain doubtfulness, as if she were not sure of being able to find the right words to tell him what she wanted. " I'm a bit afraid you may not take to Joe very much at first. He's a rather loud sort of person, whom I think it would be absolutely natural for someone like you to distrust at sight."

" What do you mean by someone like me? " Colin asked. He didn't much like the tone in which she had said it.

"What I'm trying to tell you," she said, "is that you aren't going to like Joe's face, or his voice, or his tie, or his waistcoat. But still, he's completely honest and awfully kind. *And*,"—she emphasised it—"he isn't a receiver of stolen property."

CHAPTER THREE

JOE LAKE'S TIE was of cream satin with foxhounds leaping up it. His waistcoat was of tartan, bound with leather. Ginny was right, Colin liked neither of them. At the same time, he found it very difficult to believe that any remarkable degree of honesty and kindness lurked behind the man's animated but furtive grin and the cautious probing of his red-veined eyes.

When Ginny and Colin went round together to the sale-room, they found Joe, red in the face, and puffing, pushing at the corner of an enormous wardrobe, which his wife was telling him was in everybody's way and ought to be moved into a corner. He was a fairly big man, but not, it was plain, a strong one. There was a soft layer of fat all over him, his wide shoulders sagged and his chest was hollow. He had very little of his fair hair left and deep lines ringed the thick flesh round his neck, yet there were hardly any lines on his flat-nosed, padded-looking face. The smile that he gave when he saw Ginny and Colin at the door merely drew his cheeks into pleats, which then vanished completely, as if they had only been pressed for a moment into a sponge.

Coming across the room, he wiped his hands on a silk handkerchief, then held one out to Colin. It felt hot and damp. His breath was a warm blast of whisky fumes.

"Glad to see you," he said. "Glad to tell you anything

I can about this rum do. But I can't promise it'll help. I'll tell you straight, in my opinion Ginny here got her wires crossed." He put a hand on Ginny's shoulder. " No offence, darling. We all make mistakes."

" Joe," his wife said, still from the far end of the room, " that wardrobe . . ."

" Oh," said Joe. " Yes. Well, in just a minute."

" I was merely thinking," Beryl Lake said in a cool, sharp voice, smiling at Colin as she spoke, " that if Mr. Lockie would be so very kind as to lend you a hand for just a moment, you could get the thing out of the way and then I could get on with stacking this china where people can look at it."

She was a small, slender woman of about forty, very upright, dressed in a tweed suit of a rather staring shade of green. She had some heavy gold chains round her neck, and topaz ear-rings. Her hair was dark red and wound smoothly round her head. It was very beautiful hair. Her dark eyes gave Colin a look as long and direct as her husband's had been sidelong and evasive.

" I know you don't mind my suggesting it," she said.

As he went towards the wardrobe, Colin thought that it would not trouble her in the least if he did. Beryl Lake was a woman who would let no opportunities slip of making use of anyone who happened to be around. What they felt would not concern her.

" Well now," Joe said, " I really don't like to trouble you like that. I can attend to it later."

" Joe," she said.

" Oh well."

He gave a quick, sly grin, as if really he were pleased that she had arranged things so adroitly. He went to grasp the other end of the wardrobe and between them he and Colin pushed it, a few inches at a time, into a corner of the room.

"There, that's wonderful," Beryl Lake said. "Thank you so much, Mr. Lockie. Now I'll leave you in peace to talk over whatever it is you want to with Joe."

"Here, hadn't you better listen in on it?" Joe said. "You know as much about it all as I do."

"Well, I'm here if there's anything special you want to ask me, but somebody's got to get ahead with unpacking all this stuff." She gestured at some packing cases with their lids off and straw bulging out of them. "I'd take Mr. Lockie into the office, if I were you, Joe, then you won't be disturbed if people come looking around."

"Well, all right—come along, Mr. Lockie," said Joe. "You coming too, Ginny?" He led the way into a small, untidy office, plumped down in the revolving chair at the desk and left Ginny and Colin to find seats for themselves. "I can tell you where we got that picture, if that's any good to you, but if it was stolen property, there's something bloody queer been going on, because you couldn't find a more harmless old lady than Mrs. Sibbald. And I can give you the name and address of the man who bought it and that's just about all. I can't tell you a damned thing about the picture itself. I never noticed anything special about it."

"That sounds quite a lot to be going on with," Colin said. "Who was this Mrs. Sibbald?"

"She was an old lady who lived here in Oldersfield for as long as I've known the place, and that's going on ten years." Joe picked up a packet of cigarettes from the dusty top of the desk and offered them round. "From what I've heard too, she lived here much longer than that. Most of her life, I dare say. She was a widow without any children and she lived in a house out near the golf course. Medium size house, built around the turn of the century—you know the sort of place. Fifty years ago it'd have been just right for a lone widow, living on a small pension with a cook, a housemaid and full-time gardener. These days you couldn't think why she didn't sell up and move into a nice little bungalow."

" Why didn't she? " Colin asked.

" God knows. When Beryl and me were called in after she died to see what we'd give for the stuff in the house, it was all in a terrible state. She'd been living in about two rooms of the place for years and not caring what happened to the rest of it. Chunks of plaster had come down from the ceilings, drains had got blocked up and left like that and you could stick a penknife into the dry rot in the attics like into a piece of butter. And the whole place was full of junk, stuff you couldn't do anything with but burn. Believe it or not, in one room there was a set of false teeth grinning up at us from the middle of the floor. Couldn't say how long ago she'd got fed up with them and thrown them away there. Gave me the creeps. But I suppose she was used to it and felt at home there, poor old soul."

" Were there a lot of pictures in the house? "

" Heaps of 'em. Most of them we wouldn't even touch. Advised the nephew to take them into the garden and make a big bonfire. But this one you're steamed up about, and a few others, had fairly decent frames and some of the furniture was good solid stuff, though not what you can get much of a price on these days."

" Was the nephew her heir? " Colin asked.

" That's right. Not very pleased with the situation, either. Said she ought at least to have kept the house in repair, then it'd have been worth converting into flats and would've fetched a good price. I couldn't see myself why she should have bothered, when she'd only a cold fish like him to leave it to. But he didn't see that."

" Where was the picture, when you found it? "

" Far as I remember, up in the attic. But there was such a lot of stuff jammed in cupboards, under the beds and every damned where, I may have got mixed up. Beryl may remember." He raised his voice, "Hi, Beryl!"

She appeared in the doorway, a large blue and gold plant pot in one hand, a duster in the other. She had put on a pair of spectacles with brightly jewelled frames. Behind them her eyes had the opaque gleam of damp pebbles.

"Most of this lot's terrible," she muttered, looking down at the plant pot. "We were fools to take it on. We'll never shift it."

"Beryl, d'you remember whereabouts in Mrs. Sibbald's house we found that picture?" Joe asked.

"In the attic," she answered.

"That's right, that's where I thought," said Joe.

She disappeared again.

Ginny just then caught Colin's eye. She frowned at him slightly, as if she were telling him to press on with his questioning, even if it seemed to be getting nowhere. She did not want him to lose faith yet, however improbable it might sound, that the picture found in Mrs. Sibbald's attic was the same one that had been stolen with his car.

"I suppose there's no one who can tell us how and when Mrs. Sibbald got hold of the picture," he said.

"Not unless the nephew can," said Joe. "I can give you his address—it's in North London somewhere, I remember—if that's any good to you." He opened a note-book and copied something out of it on to a slip of paper.

"Here you are," he said. "That's where he lives. But it looked to me as if he hadn't been near the old lady for years. Like I told you, he was pretty disappointed with the state of things."

"Thanks—and there's the address of the man who bought the picture, if you don't mind letting me have it too," Colin reminded him.

"Greer," Joe said. "I remember that was his name. Wait a minute." He turned the pages of another note-book.

" Here we are. Edmund Greer, Hopewood House, Hopewood. That's a village about twenty miles from here, over towards East Grinstead."

" Is he someone you've known for some time? " Colin asked. " I mean, has he often bought things from you here? "

" Well, he was nosing around the saleroom for a week or two before that particular sale. We have a sale here every Thursday and he came to the one last week and bought a few things. The best things too. A nice Sheraton teacaddy we had and a Queen Anne soup-ladle. He's got a good eye all right."

" And a green face and a nasty voice," Ginny said. " A mincing, arrogant, sinister voice."

Joe burst out laughing. Swivelling his chair so that it brought him closer to Ginny, he slid an arm around her waist and gently patted her hip.

" Darling, you've got it in for him because he beat you to it, that's all. God, I was glad when you stopped pushing him up, though it was all money in my pocket. But there I was, thinking to myself, the poor girl's going bonkers, where are she and Harriet going to put their hands on money like that? Didn't occur to me, naturally, you'd got a backer."

" So you think he did know what he was doing," Colin said. " That's one of the things I wanted to find out."

He realised that his tone had suddenly become much harsher than it had any reason to be. It had something to do with the sight of that encircling arm and patting hand.

Joe snatched one of his swift glances at Colin's face, then he stared hard at the toe of his own shoe and began to jog it nervily up and down.

" Well now," he said, after giving himself time to think, and the fact that he needed time seemed to Colin the most interesting thing that had happened so far. "I can't really say anything about that. Matter of fact, I hadn't thought about it. But I see what you mean. If he knew what he was at, perhaps the picture was worth something after all. And we missed it. Threw it away, probably. Ah well, all in the day's work. You can't fool all the people all the time. Get fooled yourself once in a while." He let his arm fall from Ginny's waist and used the hand to make the gesture of smoothing back some non-existent hair from his forehead.

"How do you manage these sales?" Colin went on. "Do you sell the things on a commission basis, or do you buy them yourselves and then sell them for whatever profit you can get?"

"Sometimes one, sometimes the other," Joe said. "Depends on the customer. I generally tell them it's in their own interest to let us work on a commission basis, because you never can tell how the bidding's going to go. Apart from shows like last Thursday, you always get the day when for some reason everyone in the place seems to have set their hearts say on some lousy old lot of blankets, and the price goes rocketing up above what you'd have to pay for them new. Or the ladies—it's generally the ladies—just get out of hand. They've come there to buy something and they're bloody well going to buy something, and they bid each other up and end by going home with something they're never going to be able to use in a hundred years. But there you are, they've had their fun, which was what they really came for. Well, naturally, if we've bought the stuff outright, the original owner doesn't get any benefit out of that sort of thing, it's us who get it. And naturally, when we do buy the stuff ourselves, we aren't going to gamble on luck like that. We make an offer for what we know we can sell the stuff for, minus a bit of profit."

Joe had talked himself out of his momentary nervousness. His feet were still.

"All the same," he went on, "you get the type from time to time who doesn't want to be bothered, doesn't want to wait, wants to be shot of the whole show, put a cheque in his pocket and push off. Or sometimes they're suspicious of you, think you've got a deal on with someone who's going to be there bidding and you aren't going to push the prices up for them. Well, if that's how they are, it's all right with me. I tell 'em they'll lose by it, and they do lose by it, but they know their own business best is what I think."

"And how did you handle Mrs. Sibbald's property?" Colin asked.

Joe Lake did not answer for a moment. Then he raised his voice and shouted, "Beryl!"

She reappeared in the doorway, empty-handed this time, except for a cigarette, which she was holding between two tobacco-stained fingers. She had short, broad, work-roughened fingers, although everything else about her was delicately made.

"Well?" she said.

"Beryl, Mr. Lockie's just been asking me how we handled the Sibbald stuff," Joe said. "It was a straight sale, wasn't it? We bought the stuff."

"You know we did," she answered.

"Yes, well, that's what I thought."

"It was your idea too, so far as I remember."

"I thought it was yours."

She shook her head. "I didn't want to handle it at all."

Joe sighed. "Of course, I see what you're getting at, Mr. Lockie. You're wondering who's been the loser over this picture. And I suppose you can say Mr. Sibbald's lost most of that hundred and ten pounds we got. All the same, I treated him right. I made him a fair offer, according to what I valued the stuff at myself, and the fact may be he's well out of things with that, if it turns out there's going to be the smell of stolen property about it."

Beryl Lake looked quickly at Colin, lifting her eyebrows.

" Mr. Lockie, you aren't serious about that, are you? "

It was Ginny who answered, " *I'm* serious, Beryl."

" Darling, we know it." Beryl gave a dry laugh. " Mr. Lockie, Ginny's told us how you lost a picture somewhere up in the Highlands and she's told us she's dead sure it's the picture we sold here on Thursday. But will you tell me how that picture could possibly have got into Mrs. Sibbald's attic? Joe's been telling you about her, hasn't he? "

" Yes," said Colin.

" And about how she lived and what her house was like? "

" Yes."

" You don't have to believe him, if you don't want to. You can go round Oldersfield, asking anyone else the same things."

" I'm quite ready to believe him," Colin said.

" Then you can't be taking Ginny seriously."

With a spark in her eyes, Ginny broke in, " But the fact is, green-faced Greer paid a hundred and ten pounds for a piece of junk out of Mrs. Sibbald's attic, and Joe's just told us he thinks Greer knew what he was doing."

Beryl spread her hands helplessly. " All right, darling, he did. And Joe and I often don't. There's nothing I'm readier to admit. I'm quite ready to grant there was one quite good thing in among all the rubbish in that house and that Joe and I missed it. We probably miss things every day of the week. But I don't see how half-blind, half-dead, poor old Mrs. Sibbald got possession of a stolen painting."

" Nor do I, but I mean to find out," Ginny said. " Because you see, I *recognised* the picture. I can't explain that if you don't understand it. It's simply a fact. For four or five years of my childhood I used to spend nearly all my holidays in the house where that picture belonged. Colin and I used to play in the room where it hung. And actually it wasn't just a picture to me. It was—almost a sort of person. When I was young enough, it used to give parties and ask the other pictures to tea."

"And that's turned you into an art-expert?" There was a bite in Beryl's voice that matched the hardness of her eyes. She turned back to Colin. "Mr Lockie, Ginny's very sweet but her imagination is just a bit uncontrolled. That's your affair, however, and so's the rest of the business and Joe and I don't mind what you do about it. Go to Mr. Greer, if you want to, and if you can prove the picture's the one you lost, you'll be able to get it back. That's the law, I believe. And you can tell him from us, if you like, that he can have his hundred and ten pounds back without our kicking about it."

"That's right," Joe said. "Can we say more than that? All we want is to keep out of trouble. Of course you realise that in a job like this we're very vulnerable. We can't always know where the stuff we handle really comes from. The most we can do is be honest ourselves and hope to get by."

"We're assuming," Beryl added in a flat, deliberate tone, "you aren't actually *trying* to make trouble for us—well, just for trouble's sake."

Colin decided not to answer that. He stood up, took Ginny's arm, thanked the two Lakes and steered Ginny out.

As they started back to the Green Tree Café, he asked, "Does your friend Beryl often say that sort of thing? That last remark practically accused us of trying to blackmail them."

Ginny laughed. "Oh, that's just Beryl. It's her way

of talking. She's had a fairly hard life and it's made her suspicious. Joe's so easy going, she has to be tough."

"Well, why did she so ostentatiously keep out of the discussion, and yet stay near enough to the door all the time to hear what was going on?"

"Did she?" Ginny asked.

"Yes, I could see that bright green she was wearing through the hinge of the door."

"Oh well, perhaps she likes Joe to think he's handling things by himself. I expect she thinks it's good for him. Good for his ego, you know. Good for his pride."

"I've a feeling the ego of your friend Joe can take care of itself."

Ginny gave a sigh. "Whenever people say, ' *your* friend So-and-So,' it's always meant to be unpleasant. They always mean, 'So-and-So, whom I can't bear the sight of and whom I utterly despise you for liking.' Well, I knew you wouldn't like Joe. All the same, you're wrong about him. He's perfectly honest, even if he does say so himself. His good name means a lot to him." They had reached the door of the café. "Let's have some tea now, and decide what to do next."

"Is there anything to be done?"

"Then you don't believe I'm right about the picture. You don't think it's the same one."

"How could it be, Ginny?"

"You could at least go and see Greer." She pushed open the door. "Anyway, come in and let's talk it over."

They had tea, as they had had lunch, beside the electric fire in her mother's basement room. There were more customers in the café than there had been at lunch time, and more tramping backwards and forwards over their heads. Ginny said that she would soon have to go and help as they were just reaching the busiest part of the day.

"The market packs up in half an hour," she said,

" and lots of them come in then for high tea." She poured out a cup of tea and pushed it towards Colin. " If you'd stay on until to-morrow, when I shan't be so busy, I could go with you to see Greer. And then I think we ought to talk to the Sibbalds."

" The Sibbalds? In London?" Colin had been looking out of the barred window at the ankles of the people going by on the pavement above. He had been thinking about the interview with the Lakes. He turned to look curiously at Ginny. " This whole affair seems to mean a great deal to you," he said. " I don't quite understand it."

Under his gaze, her thin cheeks reddened.

" The question is, shall I come with you? " she asked.

" Can you leave this place for the day? "

" Oh yes. For one thing, Mother gets back to-morrow."

" Then come, if you want to."

" Only the trouble is," she said, " you've begun to suspect I'm getting you into something or other for some mysterious reason of my own—something you're afraid you won't like, when you find out what it is."

" I hadn't got as far as that, Ginny," he said. " I'm simply puzzled."

" I know. And I realise there's something awfully queer about the way the picture's turned up where one of the very few people who could be counted on to recognise it was bound to see it. That *is* what you've been thinking about since we got back from the Lakes', isn't it? You think it's just too much of a coincidence to have happened quite by chance."

" For heaven's sake," he said, " coincidences happen. They're always happening."

But later that evening, in the room that he had taken at the Black Swan, he pondered those words of Ginny's. For of course he did not like coincidences. He thought them dangerous things, to which you should allow as little

credit as possible, otherwise you could be sure that the
very thing which you had dismissed as pure chance, pure
accident, and altogether irrelevant, would turn out to be
the one thing that would have made sense of the mess of data
which you had been nearly killing yourself for weeks, or
months, or years to interpret.

Getting into bed, he turned out the light and lay gazing
up at the faintly stirring pattern on the ceiling made by the
shadow of some trees in the now quiet street. He frowned
in the darkness. He thought of the strange intensity with
which Ginny seemed to want him to believe, against all
reason, that the picture in the Lakes' Saleroom had been the
picture stolen from him in Argyll. He thought also of the
curious matter of John Clitheroe.

Ginny had said that it had been through a man called
John Clitheroe, who was in the department of History, or
Economics, or something like that at Edinburgh University,
that she had known where to look for Colin when she
wanted him. But, before going to bed, Colin had looked
through the pages of his University Diary, which gave the
names and addresses of all the University staff, and had
found no John Clitheroe there. Not in History, not in
Economics, or anywhere else.

So what was really behind it all? But sleep was creeping
up on Colin. Images were becoming far clearer in his mind
than ideas. A road seemed to stretch before him, a curving
road, disappearing into a dark distance. He could hear
seagulls crying. The last streaks of a sunset were shining
in a sky of broken clouds. A blur of copper lay on the surface of a slate-grey sea, seen between hills covered with
rusty bracken.

He found himself getting out of his car. He was going
towards a figure lying in the middle of the road. He was
bending over him. As he did so, the man moved a little.
His eyes opened and looked into Colin's.

As always happened when Colin found himself going through this scene on the edge of a dream, he saw the man's face surprisingly clearly. It was a puffy face, with thick, dark eyebrows and eyes that gleamed with ugly brilliance between puckered lids. Colin always thought at that point that if he ever saw the man again, he would know him. But then he slid down into sleep, and in the morning, when he woke, he would recall hardly anything about the man who had lain there in wait for him. . . .

CHAPTER FOUR

THE NEXT DAY was warmer, sunny and wind-still. Mixed with the protesting roar of the traffic trapped in the narrow main street, there was an exultant singing of birds.

Colin arrived at the door of the Green Tree Café at ten o'clock and was greeted by Ginny, who was wearing a short sheepskin jacket, a tweed skirt and a bright red sweater. Her face was bright and eager, as if she were looking forward to what they had agreed to do.

"We'll borrow Mother's car to go to Hopewood," she said. "It'll be nice on a morning like this. It's a very pretty village and it's got a nice pub. We might have lunch there."

Thinking that there was something very attractive about the thought of driving through Kentish lanes, where there would be catkins quivering in the hedges and celandines in the ditches, to have lunch with Ginny in some thatched and half-timbered Kentish pub, where the beer would be much better than it ever was in Scotland, Colin answered, "All right, let's go. But let's forget about Greer, Ginny. I've been thinking it over. It can't be the same picture. Let's forget the whole thing."

"Oh, we can't do that," she said. "One can't just drop things in the middle."

"Sometimes it's a pretty good idea," Colin said, "when there's no point in going on."

"No, I've seen too much of that sort of thing." The set of her jaw was stubborn and she led the way to a red Mini-Minor parked in a corner of the square.

It took them about half an hour to reach Hopewood. The only Kentish lanes they drove along were those of a three-lane highway, busy with the week-end traffic from London. But the village was as pretty as Ginny had said. It was a cluster of weather-boarded cottages built around a triangular green, with a screen of great chestnuts protecting it from the main road and a duck-pond in one corner. The fat, sticky buds on the chestnuts were beginning to split open, showing the crumpled tufts of new leaves. Some pussy willow by the pond caught the light of the morning with a sheen of silver.

"We'd have been sensible to ring up first in case the man's away or refuses to see us," Colin said as Ginny stopped the car in front of a squat church that stood among yews in a trim churchyard.

"I've done that already—at least, I got Joe to do it for me," Ginny said. The warmth of the sun made her unbutton her sheepskin jacket. "I thought it would sound better coming from him than from either of us. He said Mr. Greer sounded a bit stiff, but told us to come along if we wanted to."

"You'd probably sound stiff too if you were rung up and told you'd been buying stolen property," said Colin. "You realise we aren't going to get anywhere with him, don't you?"

"He told Joe you could look at the picture, and that's something, isn't it? And, as a matter of fact, Joe didn't say anything about its having been stolen." They had started to walk along the edge of the green, looking for Hopewood House. " He didn't say anything either about giving Greer his money back, and for Joe's sake, I don't think we ought to mention it except as a last resort."

" Meaning we try first to see if Greer will peacefully part with the thing for nothing? "

Something in his voice made Ginny give him a quick glance. " Colin, you'd really much sooner not go ahead with this thing, wouldn't you? Well, if you like, I'll see him on my own. Only of course it won't be the same thing. It's your seeing the picture that's important."

" No, it's all right, Ginny, I'm coming," Colin said. " But for some reason I wish you hadn't brought Joe into it."

" But Mr. Greer knows him a little and it'll save us a lot of explaining. And you're all wrong about Joe. I tell you, you can trust him."

" Somehow I can't feel your confidence," Colin answered with a dubious smile.

" I'm afraid you aren't a very trusting person, are you? " she said. " You know, a thing I generally dislike very much is making silly generalisations about nationality and race and so on—they're usually about a hundred years out of date, if there was ever any truth in them at all—but you really do strike me as a fairly distinct specimen of the cautious Scot."

He burst out laughing. " Some time I'll tell you how you strike me, Ginny! "

" I think I know how I strike you," she answered sombrely. " Me and my friend Joe. We needn't go into it."

They had reached the far end of the green. A passing villager, pointing at a house, told them that that was where Mr. Greer lived. Built right at the edge of the road, without any garden surrounding it, it gave a curious impression of having turned its back on the village, perhaps in an ambition to be mistaken for a small castle, or even a prison. For there was only one small door opening on to the road, and there were only two narrow windows at different heights to break the grey severity of the stone walls.

"I'm glad he knows we're coming," Colin said. "I shouldn't much care to have to take the place by storm."

"Perhaps there's another way in round the other side," said Ginny. "Let's go and see. It would be a tactical error to arrive at the back door."

They went on along the road. A high wall, they found, was built straight out from the side of the house, and a little way down the road there were wrought-iron gates. Through the gates they saw lawns of extreme neatness, dotted with uninteresting evergreens, and an impeccably kept gravel drive. On this side the house had a commonplace Victorian façade, with tall sash windows and a pompous doorway.

"He's got money," Ginny said as they started up the drive, "and he doesn't like people."

Colin agreed. Only money could keep the place as perfectly, lifelessly trim and only a man who valued privacy above almost everything else would choose to live in a house that had such a bleak air of detachment from its surroundings.

Ginny rang the bell and after a moment the door was opened by an elderly manservant in a white jacket. He had white hair, thick, white eyebrows and suspicious eyes. He looked as if he had to battle with a powerful impulse to tell them to go away instead of letting them in. For why should anyone come to that door, his tight mouth implied, but someone who was selling vacuum cleaners or collecting for charity? However, he had apparently been told to expect them and not to turn them away. Taking them up a wide staircase with heavily carved banisters, he showed them into a room on the first floor.

It was a long room, with three tall windows overlooking the garden. It had a high moulded ceiling, a big fire burning in a marble fireplace like an ancestral tomb, curtains of yellow velvet and walls covered in a dark red embossed paper. There were a great many pictures on the walls in gilded frames. Colin had only to go two steps into the room to recognise the portrait of Ginny's Decayed Gentlewoman hanging among them.

At the same time he saw a man get up from one of the armchairs by the fire. He was of medium height and solidly built, with a hint of muscle under the well-cut dark suit and the layer of middle-aged plumpness. His face was not actually green, as Ginny had described it, but it was faintly shiny and had a waxen pallor and smoothness.

He came to meet Ginny and Colin, holding his hand out. He leant slightly backwards as he walked, which made him look as if he were doing his best to hold back from the human contact which his hand had been schooled to endure. He did not attempt a smile.

" I can't pretend I understand why you want to see me," he said, " but I'll be glad to give you any help I can. I hope you'll take a glass of sherry with me. I generally take a glass of sherry at this hour."

His voice was high and flat. The vowels were thinly fluted, the consonants sharp as knives. It sounded strangely old, far older than the man to whom it belonged, which made it seem unnatural. It must have been deliberately cultivated, Colin thought, to satisfy a vanity of some strange kind. He agreed with Ginny that it was not a nice voice.

" It's good of you to see us," he said. " It's about the picture you bought at Lake's saleroom on Thursday. I believe Mr. Lake told you that."

" He did, he did. The lady yonder." Still leaning slightly backwards, resting one hand in the small of his back,

Edmund Greer turned to where the picture hung. "She's very charming. A sweet creature. And I shan't be at all surprised, when we get her cleaned up, if she turns out to be even nicer than we think." He glanced at Ginny. "So I forgive you, young lady, for pushing me up when I thought I was going to get her for next to nothing. I even enjoyed our little contest. What I don't understand, however, is what Lake's up to now. He got a far bigger price for her than he'd any reason to expect. What's he worried about?"

"There's a question," Colin said, embarrassment making his speech more abrupt than he intended, "if he'd actually any right to sell her. Miss Winter's convinced the picture is one that belongs to some relations of mine. That's why she was bidding for it. Like you, she expected it to fetch next to nothing and she was trying to get it back for us without starting a hue and cry about stolen property."

Mr. Greer went on gazing at the painting. "Stolen property. Well, well," he said softly.

"If it's the same picture," Colin said.

"I see, I see. And here am I, quite in love with her . . . Take a good look at her, however, Mr. Lockie. Make up your mind about her. Then come and have a drink and let us discuss the situation in an atmosphere of calm and reason."

He waved Colin towards the picture and still sloping backwards, walked off to the fire, before which the man-servant was setting out a decanter and glasses.

Such good-humour made Colin feel more embarrassed than ever. To give himself a little time to think, he went close to the picture and made a show of studying it. But there was really no need for him to do so. What he had expected before coming into the room he was not sure—probably that the picture would have very little true resemblance to the one that had hung at Ardachoil—yet after only one look he had known that it was the same one. Like Ginny, he had recognised it as he would have recognised a friend. The very dirt on the canvas and the pattern of the cracks in the varnish were part of a personality that he had known since childhood.

The woman in the picture was no great beauty. Her face was broad-featured, middle-aged and weary. It was turned half aside, with the eyelids lowered and the lips pursed in an expression of worried sadness. She was wearing a plumed black hat that shaded one side of her face, pearl drops in her ears and an enormous ring on the first finger of one of the hands that were limply crossed at her waist. There was something about her, an air of well-meaning, suffering earnestness that had always reminded Colin of the eldest of his aunts—only Aunt Clara would never have worn such a low-cut dress, or such an ostentatious ring. Other days, other ways, however. What colour the hair or the dress in the portrait had once been could hardly be guessed at, for along with the face and bosom of the unknown woman, who had taken on a tone of discouraged brownish yellow, and whatever there might be in the background, behind her head and sloping shoulders, it had quite disappeared into dingy darkness.

"Well?" Behind Colin there was a clink of glass as Mr. Greer put the stopper back into the decanter. "Have you made up your mind about her?"

Colin turned away from the picture and went towards the fireplace. Ginny followed him. It struck him that she was deliberately staying in the background, leaving all initiative to him.

"It's extraordinarily difficult to answer," he said as Mr. Greer handed them glasses of sherry. "I think it's the same picture. I'm almost completely certain of it. But I'm not an expert."

"Ah, well," Mr. Greer murmured mildly, as if commiserating with him.

"And if Lake's story is true of how he got hold of it, I don't see how it can be the same picture."

"Lake looks a pretty average scoundrel," Mr. Greer said. He leant backwards over the fire, resting his shoulders against the black marble mantelshelf. "I imagine you needn't take any story of his too seriously. What is it, by the way?"

"He says he bought up the contents of a house in Oldersfield that had belonged to a Mrs. Sibbald. She was an old woman who'd been living in about two rooms of the house and letting everything else go to pieces. The picture was in the attic, along with a lot of junk."

"Sibbald?" Mr. Greer shook his head. "The name doesn't mean anything to me. But I don't go into Oldersfield very often. I've only recently discovered the Lakes and their Thursday sales. It's worth watching the place, I've found, for the oddment that's escaped the eye of the dealers. When was your picture stolen?"

"About two years ago."

"Tell me how it happened."

"I had it in my car," Colin said. "I was held up and the car was stolen."

"How extremely unpleasant. I hope you weren't injured. It was somewhere in this neighbourhood, was it?"

"No, that's just it—it was on the west coast of Argyll."

Mr. Greer gave a sharp laugh. "Ah, then I quite see your difficulty, Mr. Lockie. To have travelled from there to Mrs. Sibbald's attic would be a very remarkable adventure for the lady. Such a pointless adventure too, it would seem. What about the police? What effort did they make to trace her?"

"I think they took all the usual steps, whatever they are.

They never found any trace of my car, and when they caught up with the two men they thought had taken it—they'd escaped from Barlinnie a day or two before—they denied having had anything to do with it. The police were still convinced they had, but they never proved anything."

" I see. May I ask what the lady was doing in the car? "

In spite of Mr. Greer's good humour, Colin was beginning to feel irritated by his coy-sounding way of referring to the painting as if it were human.

" I was taking her—the picture—to Edinburgh for cleaning," he said.

" For some relations of yours, did you say? "

" Yes. I don't know much about its history, but I think it had been in the family for a fair time."

" Were they very distressed at the loss? "

" Not excessively." They had in fact been very much more concerned at the damage to Colin, than at the theft of the picture.

" That sounds as if they didn't consider her particularly valuable," Mr. Greer said.

" I don't think they did."

" Yet sending her away to be cleaned—that almost sounds as if they thought she might have a certain value."

" Oh, I don't know," said Colin. " The mere fact that it had come down to them from their parents and grandparents would have made them treasure it."

" Well, they'd have treasured her more, *very* much more, if they'd had a certain idea about the dear creature that I've got at the back of my mind. No—" Mr. Greer held up his hand as Ginny started to speak. " No, I won't say anything about my little idea, because I could be so very wrong. And besides, we're almost certain, aren't we, that it isn't the same picture? So it really doesn't concern Mr. Lockie's aunts at all."

" What I was going to say, Mr. Greer," Ginny said,

"is that Joe Lake's ready to pay you back the hundred and ten pounds you paid if you'll let Mr. Lockie have the picture back."

"That's very kind of Mr. Lake, Miss Winter," Mr. Greer said dryly. "He's begun to have ideas too, has he? He thinks perhaps he can get rather more than a hundred and ten pounds if he has another chance."

Colin saw a change come over Ginny's face. It was one that he had noticed once or twice before. All of a sudden it ceased to be the ingenuous face of a rather immature girl and become the knowledgeable face of a woman who was accustomed to taking blows from life and was ready to hit back with all her strength and cunning.

"Joe merely wants to keep out of trouble," she said. "That's the only idea he's had. He'll return you what you gave for the picture, and then I'm sure Mr. Lockie will pay Joe what *he* gave for the picture. Then Mr. Lockie will return it to its rightful owners and that will be the end of the matter. The police needn't be brought in at all."

"But my dear young lady, who's talking about the police?" Mr. Greer asked. "I'm the rightful owner of that picture."

"Not if it can be proved that it's the picture that belonged to Mr. Lockie's aunts," she said.

"Even then, I'm afraid." Greer gave another tolerant smile. He looked up at the picture. "There she is and there she stays," he said gently. "I love her far too much to part with her."

"If you want more than the hundred and ten pounds—" Ginny began.

He cut in, "I want more. Much, much more. Far more than you or Mr. Lockie or Joe Lake can offer. And I really think it's time to drop the subject. May I offer you a little more sherry?"

"No, thank you." Ginny put her glass down on the tray.

"Mr. Greer, have you thought that if that's the picture we think it is, you may have to give it up without getting anything back for it at all?"

"Oh no. No, not at all." He refilled his own glass. "People have such confused ideas about the law. I bought that picture in perfectly good faith on the open market. The open market—that's the point." He gave a chuckle, the kind that a man gives when he is unexpectedly charmed by the perfection of some purely intellectual discovery. "It's most amusing really. I might so easily have bought her in some hole-and-corner junk shop and then of course you'd have been right and I'd have been delighted to get my hundred and ten pounds back. But my amazing good fortune is that I really and truly bought her in the open market. So she's mine, whatever her shady past may have been, poor sweet."

Ginny turned to Colin with a puzzled look.

He said, "I don't understand, Mr. Greer."

"Then consult your lawyer, Mr. Lockie. Ask him about market overt. I'm sure he'll support what I've been telling you."

"You mean that if you buy something that's been stolen in what you call the open market, the original owner can't get it back?"

"Just so."

"Even," said Ginny sharply, "if he can *prove* it's been stolen?"

"I'm afraid I'm not certain of the details," Mr. Greer replied. "I've known of this odd quirk in the law for some time—it's something very ancient, I believe—but I've never imagined I might one day be glad to take advantage of it."

"Glad!" Ginny's eyes blazed. "Yes, you *are* glad. I see that. Thank you for making your attitude so plain, Mr. Greer. We now know where we are."

" But don't just take my word for it," he said. " Consult your lawyer. Please do."

" Oh, you may be quite sure we'll do that." She turned abruptly to the door.

Mr. Greer hurried to open it for her.

" Miss Winter, don't take this too badly," he said. " I know that bidding at auctions always rouses the worst passions and it's very painful indeed to have to admit defeat—particularly when one begins to realise that one didn't quite know what one was bidding for. But I'm sure you'll be lucky another time."

She did not answer. Her slight body was stiff with anger as she went down the stairs. Colin followed her. The man-servant was waiting at the bottom, holding the door open already, as if he could not hustle them out fast enough.

CHAPTER FIVE

OUT IN THE ROAD, Ginny burst out, " I'm sorry, Colin—I'm terribly sorry! "

There was a shake in her voice which made Colin afraid she was near tears.

" Whatever for? " He put an arm round her shoulders. " You did all you could."

" But to have let you in for that! To make you go and see that horrible man, when you didn't even want to! I knew from the sale I was going to hate him, but that he'd be quite so loathesome . . ." She seemed to feel a dreadful responsibility for having inflicted on Colin the horror of meeting Mr. Greer. " I do so hate hating people. And losing my temper. It always makes me feel ill. I'm feeling just a bit sick now."

" Then it sounds as if we ought to go to that nice pub you

talked about and have a stiff drink of something," said Colin.

As they walked on and he let his arm drop, she put her own through it.

"I don't understand how you can stay so calm," she said. "You don't seem angry at all. Yet that *was* our Decayed Gentlewoman, and what's more, he knew it was."

"As a matter of fact," Colin said thoughtfully, "I'm probably as angry as you are, even if it doesn't show." He was, as it happened, rather surprised at the strength of his own anger. It wasn't a habit of his to lose his temper easily. Normally it only happened once or twice a year, and then it was generally with himself, for some such thing as spoiling a month's work by a simple act of forgetting to turn some switch or other. "I agree with you he believed that picture was stolen property, or anyway, he wanted to. He liked the idea."

"He loved it, he's sitting there revelling in it," Ginny said. "He loved the thought of this market overt business, whatever it was. He loved the thought of using the law to get round the law."

"I wonder if he can possibly be right about that," Colin said. "I've always thought that if you accidentally bought something that had been stolen and the real owner turned up and wanted it back, it was just your bad luck. I thought you had to give it up for nothing."

"I know—so did I. So the Lakes' offer to buy the picture back struck me as pretty generous."

"About that," Colin said, "why did you mention it, Ginny? I thought you'd decided it wouldn't be fair to Joe."

"Well, I felt fairly certain Greer would refuse it, and I had a sort of idea it might make him come into the open about what he thought the picture was—which it did, up to a point. He showed us he thought it was something really valuable."

They had just reached the pub. Its bulging walls were as half-timbered as Colin had imagined them. Its roof was thatched and its small leaded windows were filled with bowls of daffodils and pussy willow. As they went in, Ginny said that the best thing for settling her stomach when her nerves were upset was always whisky and Colin suddenly decided he felt like following her example. Ordering the drinks and a plate of sandwiches, they sat down at a table by one of the windows, and Ginny at once picked up the thread that she had dropped.

"But what could the picture be, Colin? Don't you know anything about its history?"

"Very little," he said. "I was always told it's one of the things my grandfather managed to hang on to when they had to sell the house in Edinburgh—it's a nursing-home now—to pay his father's gambling debts. But I've always had a feeling the whole story was a bit of a legend. I've never quite believed in the gambling, or the debts, or the splendour of the Edinburgh house. I shouldn't be at all surprised if one of the aunts really picked up the picture in some antique shop and made up the family history to go with it."

"Well, I wonder . . ." Ginny looked towards the window and her eyes grew dreamy. "Her clothes are Charles I, you know. And if Greer's right that the picture's valuable, and not just a copy of something, d'you think— d'you think just possibly . . .? No, I know it couldn't be." She sighed and drank some whisky. After a moment it seemed to give her courage to continue her dream. "I was thinking about Van Dyck. Don't laugh."

Colin couldn't help it.

After frowning at first, she joined in. "All the same, why not? Things like that do happen sometimes."

"She's much too meaty for a Van Dyck," Colin said. "No, let's not go quite crazy about this. Let's think out what we're going to do about this market overt business."

"You do want to do something, do you—even if she isn't a Van Dyck?"

"You bet I do!"

"Well, the only thing then is to consult a lawyer."

He agreed. "In London, I suppose. That means I'll have to stay over the week-end."

"Can you do that?" Ginny asked. "Haven't you got to give lectures or something?"

"No, the term's finished."

He would, however, have to telephone Bob Forsythe later in the day and ask him to take the culture labelled 2 out of the refrigerator and put it in fixative.

Unluckily, thinking of Bob Forsythe was a reminder of John Clitheroe, whose name Colin had not been able to find in his University Diary. Oughtn't he to question Ginny about him?

But Ginny had her dreaming look again, and even if all it meant was that she was on the trail of an entirely imaginary Van Dyck of fabulous value, it lit her face from within with a veiled sort of glow, which made Colin's heart suddenly lurch. He would have hated to say anything that took that look from her face.

They drove back to Oldersfield presently, discussing when to go to see the Sibbalds. Immediately, Ginny said. But when they reached the café, a woman who was talking to a Miss Heavens as they came in, turned, saw Colin, gave a shriek, ran to meet him and wound her arms round his neck in a strangling, highly scented embrace. When he recovered from it, he learnt that it was Ginny's mother.

She was very much as Colin remembered her, a vigorous, hearty-looking woman, with big breasts straining at a black woollen jumper, well corsetted hips under a tight black and white tweed skirt, several glittering strings of crystal beads round a short, plump neck, a pair of very solid calves and good ankles.

She looked to him no older than she had when he was a boy. She had seemed quite middle-aged then, yet middle-aged was all that she was now. If a few more grey hairs had appeared among her brown ones, or lines on her round, vague, amiable face, he was not aware of them.

The only thing that struck him as different from his memory of her, and it struck him at once, even before she swept him and Ginny downstairs to her basement sitting-room, was that this was a very nervous woman, whose excited, chattering welcome covered extreme tension. He did not know if it was a chronic nervousness, which he had been too young to notice before, or the result of something that was weighing badly on her mind at the moment. Whichever it was, while he was doing his best to answer her questions about his family and himself, he could tell from the fixity of her gaze and the animation with which she kept nodding her head, that she was taking in hardly a word of what he was saying.

Ginny had become almost completely silent since meeting her mother. Wandering about the room, she made a rather absent-minded effort at tidying up the shoes, stockings, blouses, scarves and jewellery that had erupted out of Harriet Winter's suitcases.

At last she interrupted, " Mother, how did you manage to recognise Colin so quickly? Who told you he was here? "

Harriet stopped in mid-sentence. She stubbed out the cigarette that she had been smoking in gasping little puffs, reached for another and said, " Beryl popped in for a moment. She saw my taxi and came round . . . Darling, do please leave my things alone! " Her voice went shrill. " I'll unpack properly presently. I just opened up my cases to find the Heavens' presents for them. I got them some enchanting embroidered doo-dahs that they can use as antimacassars, or table-runners, or just put away in a drawer and treasure, if they want to—actually, I couldn't think what on earth to bring them, but of course one has to bring something. And I've brought you something too. If you'll just leave things for the present, I'll dig it out by and by."

Ginny dropped a clanking charm-bracelet back into one of the suitcases and closed the lid on it. " Did Beryl tell you what Colin's doing here? "

"She may have, darling. Yes, of course she did. Something about a picture that was stolen turning up here. Perfectly amazing, isn't it? I mean, that it should have turned up here, of all places? And fancy you remembering it. But I'm afraid I didn't listen to Beryl very carefully. She seemed very angry about something, while I was thinking how wonderful to see Colin again and hear all about darling Dolly. She was always such a pet. I loved her. To tell you the truth, Colin, Clara and Phyllis always scared the lights out of me, and I'm sure they did Dolly too. I always wished I could get her away from them. Not that Clara and Phyllis weren't sweet too, but such prim, puritanical, Scotch old maids—pardon me, Scottish!—and Dolly was meant to be something quite different. She'd a love of life, she was a real sport. We'd never have made friends otherwise, of course. Poor, dear, old Dolly, how I'd love to see her again."

"Mother," said Ginny, seizing a moment when Harriet paused to puff at her cigarette, " have you ever heard anything hereabouts about a man called Greer? "

"Greer? I don't think so, darling. Colin, now tell me——"

"Not even from Beryl just now? "

"Oh, from Beryl? I may have. Yes, I believe I did. I think she did just mention him. Or it may have been someone else. I really wasn't paying any attention. I was trying to tell her a little about my marvellous trip, but as usual she was only thinking about her own affairs. And that's all you seem to be thinking about too." Harriet's face went mournfully reproachful. "You haven't asked a single question yet about how I enjoyed myself, or even what the weather was like, or whether I met any nice people. And as a matter of fact, I did. The man in charge of us was one of the most charming people I've met for a very long time. He was truly cultured, he knew a tremendous amount about all the buildings and pictures, yet he wasn't at all solemn about them, he was a really cheery soul, and he liked me and he said he'd like to come to Oldersfield sometime. But you just aren't interested."

With a smile, Ginny sat down beside her mother and took her hand.

"I'm sorry," she said. "I am. Go on and tell me about all the other nice people."

Harriet leaned towards Ginny. For a moment she rested her cheek against her shoulder.

"It doesn't matter," she said. "I'm glad to be home, that's the main thing. I'd a wonderful time, but still it's nice to be home. All the same, I'm sure he really liked me, it wasn't just a case of doing his job."

"I'm sure it wasn't."

Harriet gave an unexpectedly hard laugh. Sitting up again, yawning, she reached for another cigarette.

"Don't overdo it," she said. "I know what you're really thinking—and Colin too. Well, never mind. Nobody wants to listen to travellers' tales. But I did enjoy myself."

"I want to hear it all," Ginny said, "only tell me something first, because Colin has to go back to London. Have you ever heard of something called market overt?"

"Oh, darlings, Colin isn't going back to London—what nonsense!" cried Harriet. "He's staying the week-end—

of course he is. By the way, where are you staying, Colin?"

"At the Black Swan," he told her. "But I really have got to go back——"

"Impossible, utterly impossible—I won't let you go! I haven't asked you a tenth of the things I want to know. And I haven't even started to give you all the messages I want you to take back to Dolly. How I'd love to see the old girl again. And she—she might be glad to see me. After all this time, I mean." Her voice wobbled uncertainly. "I suppose you couldn't fix it? Couldn't you persuade her to come and stay with you in London?"

"Colin doesn't live in London," Ginny said. "He lives in Edinburgh."

"Oh," said Harriet. "Yes, I believe I heard that somewhere. My poor memory!"

"But we have to go to London to see the people Joe bought the picture from," Ginny went on. "Then we want to see a lawyer about market overt."

"Market overt? What the hell *is* this market overt you keep talking about?"

"That's just what we want to know," said Ginny.

"Anyway, you won't be able to see a lawyer till Monday morning."

Ginny nodded. "That's true, of course."

"Oh yes, it's true, but the trouble is, now I'm home, you simply can't get away fast enough," said Harriet bitterly. "All the way home I've been thinking for once we'll have a few days together. But first it's Colin who has to go away at once, then you let on you're going away too ... Oh well."

The result was that Colin stayed another night at the Black Swan.

In the evening he asked Ginny and her mother to dinner there. Harriet arrived in a sleeveless dress of black and gold jersey, Ginny was in the tweed skirt and red jumper that she had worn all day. The presence of her mother seemed completely to have changed her. She had become tired-eyed and silent and was holding herself in all the time.

It roused an odd protectiveness in Colin. He wanted her to stand up openly to her chattering fool of a mother and yet he was moved by the fact that she would not. After two martinis Harriet had lost all desire to hear about her old friend Dolly, or about Colin, or about what Ginny had been doing while she was away. She only wanted to take them step by step through her holiday in Spain, with special attention paid to every attractive man she had met during the fortnight.

When they were sitting over coffee in the lounge, Joe and Beryl Lake came in. They showed great surprise at finding the Winters there. They themselves had just dropped in, they said, for a quiet drink. Colin was not in the least convinced. He was sure that they had come looking for him and Ginny.

"Tell us how things went with Greer," Joe said, after insisting on buying drinks for everyone. Nursing a glass of brandy in both hands, he gave Colin one of his bright, evasive glances. It was like the sudden sally of a scouting force, making a swift reconnoitre of the ground before them, then darting back to cover. The cover, in this case, was Harriet. Joe seemed to feel safe continuing to look at her.

"You did see him, didn't you?" Beryl said.

She was wearing a plain grey dress with an ornate collar and ear-rings of jet. The light from the lamp behind her gave the shine of copper to her dark red hair. She was a far better-looking woman, Colin thought, than he had realised in the morning.

"We expected you and Ginny round this morning, Mr. Lockie," he said. "I left a message with Harriet, asking you to look in. It may not have occurred to you, but it's of some importance to us to know what's going to happen."

" Oh God, that message ! " Harriet's fingers went to the crystal beads at her neck and entangled themselves helplessly amongst them. " Darling, I'm so sorry, I don't think I ever gave it. Meeting Colin like that after all these years, there was so much else to think about. And of course so much else besides about my trip. It was really a perfectly wonderful fortnight, everything so well organised and the most marvellous man in charge of us. I don't think I told you——"

" Never mind," Beryl interrupted in her cool, sharp voice. " Mr. Lockie, please tell us what happened. The sum of a hundred and ten pounds, after all, is of some consequence to us."

" I'm sorry, I should have thought of it," Colin said. " But there's nothing much to report, beyond the fact that Greer doesn't mean to give up the picture."

" Except," Ginny said, coming suddenly to life, " that Colin agrees with me it's the one from Ardachoil. He's as sure of it as I am."

Beryl gave a dry laugh. " I find that very strange. And rather incredible. Quite incredible, to be frank. And if I may say so, it's rather a comfort to know Mr. Greer feels the same."

" He doesn't," Ginny said. " He's as sure as we are that he's got hold of stolen property. But he's found what he calls a quirk in the law, which he says makes it legal for him to keep it."

" Forgive me if I say I'm delighted to hear it," Beryl said.

" Only naturally we aren't taking his word for it," said Ginny.

" Oh no." Harriet's glass of Cointreau had been emptied very quickly. As she spoke, her face acquired a haggard solemnity. " You should never do that. Never, I mean, take people's word for things. It's one of the saddest things in life, I think, the way you can't take people's word for things. I'm a very trusting person, I expect people to believe me and I want to be able to believe them. But I know that's wrong. It's weak and stupid. The proper thing to do is always to get everything put down on paper. Even among friends. The thing is to go to a lawyer and get him to draw it all up properly and get it signed and everything, then you'll know just where you are." She gave a sad shake of her head, as if she were remembering all the occasions when she had not been guided by this wisdom. " You must go to Vickerman and Ogg on Monday, Colin. I'll ring up and make an appointment for you myself."

"Who are Vickerman and Ogg?" he asked.

"They're my solicitors," she answered with dignity. " And they were my father's solicitors, and they were his father's before him. They made an awful mess of things for me, of course, telling poor George he couldn't divorce his wife, whatever she'd done, simply because he was living with me at the time, when all he had to do was ask for the discretion of the court. You'd think they'd have heard about that, wouldn't you? They're very sound people, all the same. None of my family would ever go to anyone else."

" All right," Colin said, " we'll go to Vickerman and Ogg."

"Yes," she said, " you couldn't do better. Although just sometimes, you know——" It sounded as if she had to screw up her courage to confess to a heresy. " Sometimes I think about how perhaps George and I might have married if we'd gone to a different sort of solicitor. Not that it mattered to me. I just wanted George, any way I could have him. But it would have been so much nicer for Ginny. And then, poor darling, he was killed in the bombing . . ." Tears filled her eyes.

Joe laid a hand on her knee, patting it gently. "You're tired, angel. It's the journey. What you want is to go home and have a hot bath and a nice long sleep."

"That's right," she said. "I'm terribly tired. But I had a wonderful time in Spain. I must tell you——"

"Mr. Lockie," Beryl interrupted, "going to these lawyers sounds an excellent idea, if you don't mind spending your money. But whatever you do, Joe and I would be grateful if you'd keep us informed. May I count on that?"

"Yes, Mrs. Lake," Colin answered, "I'll remember."

"Because, like it or not, we're involved. And as I said, a hundred and ten pounds is quite a lot of money to us." She stood up. "But our offer to refund it stands, if it's going to keep us out of trouble—doesn't it, Joe?"

"What? Oh—yes. Yes, of course." He kissed Harriet's cheek and stood up beside Beryl. "Good-night, everyone."

He followed Beryl to the door. But halfway there, he turned and came back.

"I've just got to say, I don't like any of this business," he exclaimed. "I don't know what's been going on, but I don't like it. Stolen property! As if we'd ever have touched the damned thing if we'd thought it had that sort of smell to it. We run our show straight. There's never been anything said against us and that means a lot to us."

He strode off to where Beryl was waiting for him.

When the Lakes had gone, Harriet observed with a gloomy sort of wonder in her voice, "You know, I sometimes try to guess what Beryl thinks about when she isn't thinking about money. She doesn't deserve Joe. He's got a heart of gold, whatever he looks like. I'm terribly fond of him."

"Well, he was right, Mother," Ginny said. "You're tired and you ought to be home in bed. We must go."

"Yes, darling. But it's been a lovely evening, hasn't it?" She brushed away her slowly oozing tears and smiled sweetly. "Colin, it was so good of you to ask me out as well as Ginny. I've enjoyed every minute of it. And thank you for staying on. But on Monday you must go to see Vickerman and Ogg about this crooked business, whatever it is. I can't say I exactly understand it, but I'm really very worried about it. I don't like the sound of it any better than Joe. Vickerman and Ogg will understand it, though. They're a really good old firm. You can trust them absolutely."

"Yes, but to-morrow we're going to see the Sibbalds," Ginny said.

"Oh, not to-morrow, darling! Wait till Monday."

But this time Ginny was firm. As Colin saw her and her mother home to the café, they made arrangements for meeting the next day at the station.

Halfway back to the hotel, Colin remembered that he hadn't telephoned Bob Forsythe about taking that culture out of the refrigerator.

The chance of being able to track Bob down at this hour of a Saturday evening was small. The only thing was to forget about it. Colin muttered an automatic curse because of the work wasted, yet for once felt almost untroubled by the thought of it. He was thinking, as he walked along the empty main street of the old town, that he understood Ginny a good deal better now that he had met her mother again. What a life she must have had, poor girl—was still having, if it came to that. And that was a disturbing thought, because it was clear that something ought to be done about it, done soon, done decisively, before it was too late . . .

CHAPTER SIX

THE SIBBALDS' HOUSE was one of a row of semi-detached houses, all exactly alike except for the colours of their doors and window frames. Even the pattern of the stained glass panel in each front door represented the same orange sun, sinking through flaming clouds into the same blue sea. When the houses had been built, the woodwork also would have been almost as uniform, a chocolate brown prevailing. But fashion had changed. The Sibbalds' house had pink window frames, pale blue gutters and a front door of tangerine.

It was Mrs. Sibbald who opened the door to Colin and Ginny when they arrived, after having telephoned to ask if they might come. She was a short, muscular, cheerful-looking woman of about thirty-five, with curly black hair, red cheeks and a strong chin. Obviously she had a liking for the same sort of colour scheme in her dress, her wall-paper, curtains and carpets as in the paintwork outside the house. Wherever Mrs. Sibbald was, apparently, colours, pale but violent, mopped and mowed and screeched at one another, to her happy pride and satisfaction.

Mr. Sibbald, on the other hand, was a man of dim tones and very restrained manners. At a first glance his plump, spectacled face gave an impression of placid good nature, but there was petulance about his full lips and uneasy arrogance in his eyes. When his wife brought Colin and Ginny into the sitting-room, he was standing in front of the fire, holding a copy of the *Sunday Times* as if he were prepared to raise it as a screen between him and his visitors if he did not like the look of them.

Offering each of them a cold hand to shake round the

edge of the newspaper, he hurriedly sat down in the most comfortable chair in the room, and keeping the paper on his knees, fixed his gaze on his wife, showing that this odd business of letting strangers in on a Sunday afternoon was entirely her affair.

She showed herself brightly ready to answer any questions that Colin and Ginny wanted to ask her.

"Not that there's much Mr. Sibbald and I can tell you about his poor old auntie, or the things she had in that awful house," she said. "Mr. Sibbald's a very busy man. He works for the Universal Insurance Company, and that's always meant so much travelling he couldn't manage to get down to Oldersfield as much as he'd have liked. And too, he has a lot of commitments locally. He's treasurer of our branch of the Conservative Party and he does a lot of work for our church and he helps with the finances of our Operatic Society—and *that,* let me tell you, is a life work by itself." She laughed gaily. "And then there's the garden. There's always something wants doing in a garden, isn't there? So with one thing and another, sometimes it was a year or more between visits to Oldersfield. Of course, Mrs. Sibbald wasn't really a relation, just one by marriage. Her husband was brother to my father-in-law. Not that that ever made any difference to Mr. Sibbald's feeling for her."

A remark, Colin thought, that could be taken two ways.

"What I wanted to ask you about," he said, "was the picture that was found in her attic and that fetched a hundred and ten pounds at the sale in Lake's Saleroom. I wondered if you knew anything of its history."

"A hundred and ten pounds!" The mention of that sum of money brought Mr. Sibbald bouncing up out of his chair. "Are you telling me that a picture in that sale went for a hundred and ten pounds?"

"Oh, weren't you there?" Colin asked innocently.

Sitting down, Mr. Sibbald rolled his newspaper up tightly and held on to it with clenched hands. He did not answer, but there was something feverish in his gaze as he fastened it again on his wife.

She gave an uneasy laugh. " There now, I always said we ought to have gone through the house properly before agreeing to the offer Mr. Lake made us. I said, 'We can't tell what's hidden away in drawers and cupboards and all.' didn't I, dear? But to tell you the truth, Mr. Lockie, the very smell of the place put me off. Poor old woman, she'd let the whole place go to rack and ruin. She ought to have moved out years ago and gone to a nice Home, where she'd have been properly looked after. It wasn't as if she couldn't afford it. She'd quite a nice little income. It was all in an annuity, though, so Mr. Sibbald and I haven't benefited, to speak of. What was this picture you mentioned? "

" It was the picture of a woman in a plumed hat, with her hands folded in front of her and a very noticeable ring on one finger," Colin said. " It was in a rather battered gold frame."

" How big? " she asked.

" About two feet by three, I think."

She looked at her husband with a frown. " D'you remember anything like that, dear? "

" I didn't go up into the attic," he said. " I didn't like the look of the stairs. Rotten. The whole house was stinking with dry rot. A crime. It was a good property once."

" Yes, well, I admit it was a bit of a disappointment to us, the state it was in," his wife said. " We knew it was coming to us and we did think it'd be worth four or five thousand anyway, with values what they are to-day. But it's no good crying over spilt milk. Just why are you so interested in the picture, Mr. Lockie? "

" Well, it's—an interesting picture," he said. " It fetched far more at the sale than anyone expected. So I'd hoped you might be able to tell me where and when Mrs. Sibbald came by it."

"Can't tell you a thing!" Mr. Sibbald's voice was full of angry bitterness. He brought his rolled up newspaper down with a crack on the palm of one hand. "Except that Lake put one over on us. He knew what he was doing all right when he offered me a round sum for the contents. Don't tell me *he* didn't expect that picture to fetch what it did."

"Was it the only thing that got a good price?" Mrs. Sibbald asked curiously. "Were there other things that went well? I'm just wondering how badly we got stung."

Ginny answered, "I think it was the only thing that fetched much more than ten pounds."

"That's a comfort, anyway."

"I imagine the old lady didn't even know she had it," Mr. Sibbald said. "She was bent double with arthritis and if I didn't like the look of the stairs, you can bet she hadn't been up them for years. For all I know, the picture may have been up there when she and my uncle moved into the place. That's more than fifty years ago. I can't see them buying a thing like that themselves. I mean, they didn't go in for art, and if they'd done it as an investment, because they'd heard it was valuable, they wouldn't have left it rotting in a damp attic. Stands to reason. A hundred and ten pounds!" The newspaper struck again. "My guess is, it was stuck there by whoever owned the house before them."

"And I'm afraid we can't tell you about *them*," Mrs. Sibbald said with a titter, "because neither Mr. Sibbald nor I was even born then."

Colin was not interested in who had lived in Mrs. Sibbald's house before her. If the portrait of the lady in the plumed hat had been in the house for more than two and a half years, it was no concern of his.

As he and Ginny walked back to the Underground station from which they had come, she exclaimed, " They were just like Joe told us, weren't they? Respectable, cold-hearted and resentful. Did you notice Mrs. Sibbald said there was sometimes more than a year between her husband's visits to the old lady and then said how disappointed they were at the state of the house? But a house doesn't get into that sort of a state in a year or two. If they'd visited her within the last five years, they'd have known what was in store for them."

Colin nodded. " Yes, I should think we can say the Sibbalds are just what they seem to be and that probably means that what we've heard about the old lady is true too. But you see what that means, Ginny. It means they didn't put the picture up in the attic, so somebody else did— unless it was never there at all."

The line of her mouth grew hard. " Yes, Colin. At least I see what that means to you. You think Joe put it there, or anyway into the sale. But you're wrong. I keep telling you, he's a completely honest person."

" Let's think about the other possibility, then," Colin said. " Somebody else, not Joe, put the picture in the attic. Why? "

" To keep it hidden, perhaps. It would have been quite a safe hiding place. And probably quite easy to get in and out of, if Mrs. Sibbald was half paralysed and deaf and lived all the time on the ground floor."

" But that would mean that the men who held me up came all the way down to Oldersfield just to hide the picture in that attic and then—then for some reason they forgot all about it. It doesn't make sense."

" Of course, it was the picture they were after, not the car," Ginny said. " They can't have been the two men who escaped from prison."

" Which raises the question of how they knew about

it, whoever they were. I think I must go to Ardachoil in the near future and see if the aunts can tell me anything. Why *did* they suddenly want the picture cleaned? But going back to Mrs. Sibbald and her attic, why was it left there when she died? Why did someone go to all the trouble of stealing it, then forget about it?"

"Perhaps they died too," Ginny suggested.

"Or went away, thinking there was no risk of things being disturbed yet. In that case, they might decide the only thing to do was to buy it back openly at the sale."

They had just reached the Underground station. Colin went ahead to buy their tickets and because he did this, he did not notice that Ginny had not answered him. But when he turned back to her, her face was so drained of colour, so pinched about the nostrils, that it gave him a shock. But her eyes were bright with enthusiasm, or what for the moment he mistook for enthusiasm.

"Then it's been Greer from the start!" she cried. "That's wonderful—I'm so glad it's Greer! The instant I saw him at the sale, flipping his programme up and down at Joe and giving me dirty looks every time I went higher, I felt absolutely certain he was something pale and crawling that had come wriggling up out of the slime. And I don't often feel like that about people. I usually see all sorts of good points about them, even when other people warn me off."

Her eagerness was a little too shrill. Her chatter, as she and Colin walked on to the train, turned into something that sounded uncannily like the flow from Harriet to which they had both had to listen the evening before.

All the way to Charing Cross, Ginny went on elaborating her loathing of Greer. When Colin tried to talk about anything else, she came back to it. It was as if it were the only thing in life of which she felt quite sure.

Colin wanted to tell her to stop it, to warn her that she

was only driving him to think about the very thing that she was hoping she could keep out of his mind, if, with luck, it had not occurred to him yet. Because, however you looked at it, either Ginny herself or Harriet had to be the connection between Oldersfield and Ardachoil. And Harriet had gone away to Spain a fortnight before the sale . . .

He said nothing for so long that at last Ginny asked him what was the matter. He said nothing was the matter, but that he was thinking about the visit to Vickerman and Ogg. He did not say that, in the circumstances, he was not much inclined to rely on Harriet's solicitors. He only said that he had a feeling that they wouldn't get much out of them.

"If we don't, we'll try somewhere else," Ginny said. "Greer needn't think we're going to let him get away with any legal hocus-pocus."

"Yes," Colin said, "that's just what I was thinking myself."

At Charing Cross he saw Ginny on to the Oldersfield train. Her mother had managed to make her promise to return for the evening and had wanted Colin to come too, but Ginny had said that she knew he wanted to stay in London. He had thought that she did not want him to see any more than could be helped of her mother. When her train had gone, he went to a telephone. He rang up a friend of his Imperial College days, whom he still saw quite often when he came south, and asked if he knew anything about solicitors in London.

"Well, well," came the answer, "what's the trouble, Colin? Murder, divorce or drunk-in-charge?"

"It's—fraud of a sort," Colin answered hesitantly, not wanting to say any more than he must.

"Then I can take it you're the victim. Well, I've a brother-in-law who's a solicitor, if he's any use to you."

Colin got out his diary and a pencil. "What's his name?"

"Paul Dickman, of Copsey, Costelloe and Dickman. They're in Gray's Inn. I forget the number, but you'll find them in the phone book. Mind you, I don't know much about Paul's abilities. He's the sort of man who'd hate you to be able to guess at sight that he's a solicitor, but he seemed quite adroit about buying our house for us, which is the only professional contact I've ever had with him. Which reminds me, where are you staying to-night? The spare bedroom's free and Anne's just muttering in my ear that there's plenty of food in the house."

So Colin took a train to Golder's Green and spent the night with Denis and Anne Goode, passing most of the evening in an argument with Denis about the influence of the nucleus in morphogenesis. For a little while the problem of the Decayed Gentlewoman seemed to become strangely unreal and far away.

But in the morning Anne rang up her brother and made an appointment for Colin to see him at three o'clock. With a satisfied feeling that he had taken at least one step in the affair of the stolen picture that had not been somehow imposed on him by Ginny, he went to meet her.

Their appointment with Mr. Ogg was at twelve o'clock.

"You'd better do the talking," Ginny said as they went in at the street door of the firm's Holborn offices. "I'm just going to be watchful and discreet."

Following an arrow that pointed up the stairs, she started up them. Colin found himself more impressed by the atmosphere than he had expected. The staircase was a very fine specimen of Victorian public lavatory architecture. The walls were covered with dingy coloured tiles in a pattern of little paddle steamers plying across what was no doubt the Atlantic. The stone steps were worn at the edges and there was a smell of smoky staleness. The general effect was one of great respectability, for only a firm with the self-confidence of perfect probity could have afforded such an unattractive entrance.

At the top of the stairs they were met by a clerk of great age, wearing a wing collar and stiff cuffs, who conducted them along a short passage into a minute and windowless waiting-room. It smelt of musty leather and was lit by a single weak bulb, dangling from the centre of a remote and dusty ceiling. There they waited until twenty-five minutes past twelve, when at last Mr. Ogg was ready to see them.

He came to fetch them himself, suddenly throwing open the door and coming in with a large hand outstretched and giving each of them a painfully muscular handshake. He was a big bear of a man, not more than fifty, which was younger than seemed appropriate in that place. He had a square, strong-featured face and charcoal grey hair with a white pin-stripe in it, which happened just to match the suit that he was wearing. For a moment he seemed to fill the dead air of the little waiting-room with a warm, benevolent presence, with friendliness and vitality.

But the moment was soon over and the effort of having produced this impression of himself, just in case the two strangers in the waiting-room might have been worth impressing, seemed to leave Mr. Ogg slightly worn. Once he was seated behind the big desk in his roomy, book-lined office, he became merely an impatient man with an eye on the clock and his thoughts on something else, most probably lunch at his club. His geniality had disappeared like a light switched off.

When Colin began to describe the nature of the problem that had brought him and Ginny there, there was nothing responsive in Mr. Ogg's manner. He made a note or two on a sheet of paper, then, as Colin could see from where he sat, doodled pictures of fish all round them.

"Hmmmm," he said at last, neatly drawing scales in all over something that might have been a salmon. "I see. Difficult business, market overt. Yes. I doubt very much if there are any decided cases on just the point you raise. I'd have to look it up." The thought seemed to fill him with depression. He gave a pointed glance at the clock. "You say you can prove the original ownership of the picture?"

"I'm not sure that I can," Colin said. "But that isn't the point I'm raising at the moment. What I want to know is, *if* the picture bought by Mr. Greer is the one that was stolen from me, does the fact that he bought it in what he calls the open market really transfer legal ownership to him? And exactly what constitutes an open market?"

"Exactly, ah!" The salmon was acquiring fins that made it look like a flying fish. "Very difficult to tell you exactly. Roughly—you won't want technicalities—roughly speaking, it's, ah, well, a market——"

The telephone on Mr. Ogg's desk rang.

"I'm sorry," he said, picked the telephone up and spoke into it for the next ten minutes to a woman who appeared to be in trouble with a neighbour about the noise made by her very large number of dogs. The sum of his advice to her seemed to be that it was all a bad business, however you looked at it. Naturally he was very sorry for her, but what could he do?

At last he put the telephone down. "You were saying . . .?"

"We were talking about market overt," Colin said.

"Hmmmm, yes. Was it by any chance in the City of London that the sale took place?"

"I think I said it was in Oldersfield in Kent."

"Yes, so you did. It's all rather different in the City, I believe."

"It isn't in the City."

"No." The salmon-cum-flying fish was blowing bubbles all the way up one side of the paper. "Well, it sounds to me as if this man Greer you mentioned may quite possibly have a case. As I understand it, he purchased the picture in a regular market. In any case, you'd find it very difficult to bring the matter home to him. Difficult and expensive. The cost of an action would almost certainly exceed the value of the picture. Oh yes, certainly."

"But if we went to the police, wouldn't they take the action?"

"No, no." Mr. Ogg looked up at the clock with an air of hungry concentration. "You'd have to start proceedings yourselves. There's a section in the Larceny Act of 1916 which states that if anyone guilty of knowingly receiving stolen property is prosecuted to conviction by or on behalf of the owner, the property shall be returned to the owner. *By or on behalf of the owner*—that's the point. I'm sorry for you, very sorry indeed. But since you aren't even sure you can prove the picture is really the one that was stolen from you——"

The telephone rang again.

"I'm sorry," Mr. Ogg said, reaching for it again.

He was in the middle of another conversation with the same woman who was ringing up about the same dogs, and which this time threatened to go on for ever, when Colin and Ginny stole quietly out.

"Poor Mother," Ginny said as they went down the stairs past all the little paddle steamers. "I expect he was sorry for her too. No wonder my father never got his divorce. And times have changed for the worse too. In the days when her grandfather was advised by Grandfather Ogg, or it may have even been by Vickerman himself, though I've never heard anyone mention him, there was quite a lot of money in the family to advise about. Of course, the advice didn't stop it from disappearing, but I expect we got a little more attention."

They had reached the street. Ginny started towards the nearest bus stop. But Colin stood still. He took her by the arm.

"Listen, Ginny, I'm not sure if I meant to tell you this," he said, "but I've got an appointment with another solicitor this afternoon. I made it because I didn't trust your mother's solicitors and I may as well tell you, I didn't trust them because I didn't quite trust her. Now I know I don't trust them, but that's got nothing to do with your mother. I simply don't intend to let a dull, lazy bastard like that have any influence on my actions."

She was standing close to him, looking into his face. He did not know what her expression meant, except that she did not mean him to know.

He went on, "Do you want to come with me?"

"Do you want me to come?" she asked.

"Yes."

Her stiff features relaxed. But there was something subdued in her voice as she said, "Well, let's go and have lunch and you can tell me about this solicitor of yours. Look, there's a milk bar just over there. They'll have sandwiches."

"Sandwiches! By and on behalf of the owner of my stomach, let me tell you," Colin stated, "we need steak for once!"

CHAPTER SEVEN

Mr. Dickman, of the firm of Copsey, Costelloe and Dickman, was about half the size of Mr. Ogg. To make up for this, he talked twice as fast and with a shining-eyed delight in the mere act of talking which promised at least a greater value of wordage. He had short, stiff, sandy hair, arching sandy eyebrows and a small, eager, excitable face. Its dark tan did not seem quite to belong in a solicitor's office, nor did his greenish tweed suit, his rough woollen tie, or his thick-soled country shoes.

" Market overt? " he cried in a tone of incredulous joy almost as soon as Colin had begun to describe his problem. " Oh, oh, this is what I've been longing for all my life! A real honest to goodness case of market overt! More fun if I'd been called in on the other side, of course—wonderful to have a chance to defend a man's right to hang on to stolen property! A legal daydream. But still, go on, go on! "

He rubbed his hands together, his eyes shone and all his features twitched.

This unexpected explosion of enthusiasm made Colin lose the thread of his story.

Ginny picked it up. " You see, Mr. Dickman, I saw this picture in Lake's Saleroom—I saw it there on Wednesday, in with a lot of rusty old rubbish—and I got in touch with Dr. Lockie and told him it would be up for sale on Thursday and asked him if he'd like me to buy it back for him. I never dreamt it would go for more than a few pounds, I just thought he and his family might like to get it back without starting up a lot of fuss with the police."

" The actual value of the picture," Mr. Dickman said,

" doesn't affect the matter at all. No doubt you understand that."

" But if I'd thought of it being valuable," Ginny said, " I'd have gone to the police straight away. And certainly I'd have said something about it to Joe Lake. Then he'd have withdrawn it from the sale till we knew where we were and it wouldn't have got into this market overt mess."

" Yes, I see." Gripping the edge of the desk with his brown little hands, the solicitor swung his chair rapidly from right to left, his gleaming, happy gaze shifting quickly between Ginny's face and Colin's. " So you want to know a little more about the matter. Well, you can read it up for yourselves, if you're interested, in Kelly's *Outline of Criminal Law*. Wait a minute!"

He bounced out of his chair, and shot across the room and reached for a volume on one of the bookshelves.

" Here we are—sixteenth edition, published 1952." Walking up and down, he turned the pages. " Now let's see . . . Section 315. 'Fairs and markets brought together men from places so distant that in mediaeval days . . .' Well, you won't want me to read you the whole of it. What it comes to is that in those times a purchaser might know so little about the vendor, might find it so impossible to find out anything about him, that he needed some kind of protection. I mean, supposing he was some law-abiding character in a place like Oldersfield and he was offered something for sale by someone he'd never seen before from—oh, even fifty or a hundred miles away. No need to bring in anything as exotic as the Highlands. How was he to know if it had been honestly come by or not? So it was settled that if he bought it in good faith on a market day, in a place that was an established market for that particular kind of goods, he became the proprietor of the goods."

He shut the book, tossed it on to a pile of books on the floor and thudded back in his heavy shoes to his chair.

"That point's important, by the way—the market being for the particular kind of goods," he said. "If you bought, say, some nice jewellery in a corn or cattle market, you wouldn't be protected. You couldn't sell clothes at Smithfield and claim the privilege of market overt—that's been decided. There was a case in 1596 when it was held that the privilege of market overt didn't apply in the case of the sale of some plate in a scrivener's shop. I should explain, perhaps, that in the City of London a shop can sometimes be an open market, but only its ground floor. And the goods, in all cases, have to be displayed beforehand, where the public can come to look at them, and the sale has to begin and end in the market. You can't start the transaction elsewhere and complete it in the market, or vice versa. Also, it must take place between sunrise and sunset. No shady dealings in the dark." Mr. Dickman's cheerful glance settled on Ginny's face. "Is that what you want to know, Miss Winter?"

"I suppose so," she said, "though it doesn't look too good for us. This sale started at nine in the morning. It's a regular sale too—it's held there every Thursday. And they're always selling pictures. And the saleroom opens straight on to the market place. They actually display a lot of stuff outside on the pavement. That's where I saw this picture of ours."

"Remarkable!" cried Mr. Dickman, beaming. "It has a sort of beauty, hasn't it? A sort of perfection. And to think that only this morning I never dreamt that anything of the sort would ever come my way. It's so utterly unlikely, after all. There was I, on the Berkshire downs—I spent the week-end walking, I often do, I couldn't stand the office at all if I didn't—well, there was I, walking to the station, thinking gloomily this damned great metropolis was going to swallow me up again for the next five days. And all the time *this* was waiting for me!"

"What you're telling me then," Colin said, "is that Greer was right in what he told us. He did buy the picture in market overt and there's nothing we can do about getting it back."

"No, no, no!" The revolving chair swung agitatedly. "Naturally things aren't exactly as they were in 1596. I didn't mean to give you that impression. Modern facilities of intercourse have reduced the need for the sort of protection we've been talking about, so it's rather less than it used to be. Even when goods have been bought in market overt, it's possible for the original owner to regain possession of them if the thief or the guilty receiver is convicted of stealing or receiving."

"But a man isn't guilty of receiving stolen property if he doesn't know it's stolen, is he?" Colin asked. "You see, Miss Winter's convinced Joe Lake didn't know anything about how the picture got into the Sibbald attic."

"If that's true, then he isn't guilty of receiving," said Mr. Dickman.

"And they never caught the thief."

The swaying chair became still. Screwing up his features into an unreadable knot, the solicitor folded his hands behind his head and gazed at the ceiling.

"God, how glorious it was up on the downs," he murmured. "The morning sunshine, spring in the air, the birds . . . I wish I could tell you something more helpful, Mr. Lockie. But it does rather look to me, you know, as if your man Greer may have got away with it. For one thing, going to law is the most expensive pastime in the world."

"So it's a fact there's nothing we can do."

"Except that I've a sort of feeling in my bones there's something a little too perfect about all this. It's almost as if Greer must have known . . . No, that's going too far. If you could prove, however, that he did know the picture was stolen, the fact that the sale took place in market overt wouldn't help him."

"Because he'd then be guilty of resetting—I mean, receiving—himself."

"Just so, though so long after the original theft, it would be very difficult to prove. . . ." Suddenly Mr. Dickman tipped himself forward and gave Colin another of his happy, excited looks. "Resetting! That's the Scots word for receiving, isn't it? And the theft happened in Scotland. Why didn't I think of this before? Because it's all quite different in Scotland. Quite different."

"This law about market overt?"

"Yes. The trouble is, though, I don't know nearly as much as I should about Scots law. But I do happen to know that on this point it's quite different from the English. The Scots don't recognise market overt at all. As I understand the matter, if the picture remained in Scotland, your family would have retained their right to it, however many hands it had passed through since the theft and however openly and honestly it had been bought. I've an idea too there wouldn't be any question of your having to bring an action yourself. It would be a job for the public prosecutor. Well, well, what a pity we aren't in Scotland. All the same, I wonder if it mightn't be worth your while to look into it when you return home. No, I don't suppose it would, except for the interest of the thing. The sale took place in England and the picture's in England. But the whole subject's wonderfully interesting—wonderfully. Of course, now that it's too late for my advice to be any good to you, I can tell you what you ought to have done as soon as you saw the picture."

"What ought I to have done?" Colin asked.

"Helped yourself to it! Because in a doubtful situation like this, I think you'd find possession was nine points of the law."

Colin smiled, which he supposed was what was expected of him.

" Perhaps it isn't too late for that," he said, getting to his feet. " I'll think about it."

Mr. Dickman bounced up out of his chair. " But I'm serious! A man has the right to take reasonable steps to recover what he honestly believes to be his own property. That isn't stealing. If you've lent a friend a book and he can't be induced to return it, it isn't stealing if one day, when you're in his house, you put it in your pocket. So if you'd gone to Greer's house and removed the picture *before coming to me*, you could always have pleaded that that was what you'd done. But since you came to me and learnt that the ownership of the goods had been divested by the sale in market overt, you can't plead any more that you believe the picture is yours. Such a pity. But no, perhaps it isn't. Dangerous ground I'm getting on to, very."

" Mr. Dickman," said Ginny, who had not moved from her chair, although the two men were now at the door, " I believe you're advising us to burgle that house at Hopewood and then go hell for leather for Scotland."

" Miss Winter! " Mr. Dickman gave a little strangled crow of laughter. " My dear Miss Winter, it's precisely what I'm telling you not to do. Not on any account. I've just explained, you wouldn't have a leg to stand on."

" But you put it into our minds, all the same."

" Did I really? It wasn't there before? Well, perhaps not. I do get carried away by my own imagination rather easily. No reason to suppose everyone else has the same problem."

He opened the door.

Ginny still did not move.

" Mr. Dickman, I'm very sorry to have to tell you this, after all the trouble you've taken to explain things to us," she said, " but really it's all gone right over my head. I've hardly understood a single word of it."

She smiled with a caricature of her mother's manner.

" I'm not clever like Dr. Lockie," she went on. " I haven't a trained mind. I've a very slow and muddled one. And I'm afraid I'm in a complete muddle over everything you've said, except that a man has the right to take reasonable steps to recover what he honestly believes to be his own property. You put that so cleverly and well, Mr. Dickman."

At last she stood up, walked to the door and held out her hand.

" Thank you so much. Good-bye."

He took her hand. He did not let it go at once, but held it as if he were wondering what to do with it. When he relinquished it, it was with a gesture of passing on some responsibility connected with it to Colin.

Going down the stairs with them to the entrance, standing there looking out at the lawns and the great trees, he remarked, " There's sometimes an immense difference between theory and practice and almost the only advice I ever give with my whole heart is, ' Forget about it, whatever it is.' I hope that's clearly and simply put, Miss Winter. Forget it and try walking." His glance dropped to Ginny's feet, which were not as sensibly shod as his own. " Or something," he added, as he withdrew into the building.

" Or something," Ginny echoed with a laugh as they walked away. " What do you think we should do now, Colin ? "

" Sit down here for a little while," he said, stopping at a bench at the side of the walk. " It's one of the peacefullest spots in the whole of London."

" I meant," she said as she sat down, " what's the next step ? "

" Forget the whole show," Colin answered. " Dickman gave us good advice."

" It may sound good to you," she said.

" Why not to you? "

She frowned, looking away from him down the walk across the almost empty courtyard. Some pigeons had come hopping around their feet, hoping for crumbs. Over their heads in one of the tall trees a cloud of sparrows was making a great twittering. The slanting afternoon sunshine lit up the swelling buds on the twigs.

" As a matter of fact, I think you know," she said. " Not that it matters very much to me what happens to the picture. I'd like you and your family to have it back, if it's valuable, but what matters to me more than that . . ." She turned to him, looking at him with harrowed eyes. " I keep wishing I'd never seen the thing at all, or never given it a second thought and never got hold of you. But since I did stumble right into the middle of whatever's going on, I've got to find out what it is."

" Because you believe your mother's mixed up in it? "

" Don't you? "

He wanted to say that he didn't, to say it warmly and convincingly and take that look from Ginny's face. But the words stuck. To his own surprise, he heard himself asking with jerky suddenness, " Ginny, who's John Clitheroe? "

Her eyes opened wide in bewilderment. " Who's——? But I told you."

" Yes, I know." Colin's face went bright red. He was wishing desperately that there was some way of withdrawing the ill-timed question. Yet now that it was out, there was nothing to do but to plough on. " Look, Ginny," he said, taking his diary out of his pocket, " you told me John Clitheroe was someone in the History or Economics department at Edinburgh University. But if that's what he is, his name would be here, and it isn't."

"It isn't?" She reached for the diary. As she turned the pages, she did not look as if she were seeing them.

"He isn't in any other department either," Colin said, trying to keep his voice gentle, not to turn what he was saying into an attack on her. "Yet you told me he was the person who told you where I was."

"Yes," she said. "What's the date of this diary, Colin? This year's, I suppose. Yes, naturally. Do you get a new one every year?"

"Yes, of course."

"I meant, is all of it new every year? All these names and addresses?"

"Oh yes, they're kept up to date."

"Then that explains it. John's in Canada now. He went there last year. It was quite soon after he first went to Edinburgh that he told me he'd met you. Don't you remember anything about it?"

"No, but that needn't mean anything. It could have been at some meeting or party, when his name didn't register with me, for some reason, when mine did with him." He was in a hurry to reassure her, feeling profoundly reassured himself because there was such a simple explanation of John Clitheroe, because he was real. "I'm sorry I had stupid ideas about him. It was not being able to track him down here, together with not being able to work out how you and your mother ever heard about the theft of the picture, when I was sure your mother never read it in any newspaper . . . Oh, Ginny!"

She had turned away from him, was gazing away down the walk, was rigid and very white.

"Ginny, please, I'm terribly sorry," he said. "I'm a complete fool. I didn't really distrust you——"

"Sh!" she said fiercely, turning towards him again and

suddenly moving closer to him. "Don't look up suddenly, Colin, but try to get a look at the man who's just coming along. Only don't let him see you notice him."

Colin's instinct, naturally, was to look up at once. He might not have stopped himself in time if Ginny had not grasped his arm, raised her face to his with an expression of utter absorption in him, and started to talk swift gibberish.

Colin stopped it by bringing his mouth down on hers.

As he heard slow footsteps approaching, his arms went round her. He did not look up. The rigidity melted out of Ginny's body, her breath came faster. Colin had just time to wonder if quite all of it was playacting, because there was none about the way that his heart was pounding, when the footsteps drew level with them and he had to snatch a glance over Ginny's head at the man who strolled by.

He was in an old raincoat and his face was averted. By his walk and the white hair that showed under his felt hat, it was possible to tell that he was an oldish man, but not much more. Yet there was something familiar about him, something about the fringe of white hair and the set of the shoulders, moving away from them, that stirred Colin's memory. Change the raincoat for a white jacket, imagine beetling eyebrows and hard supercilious eyes. . . .

"It's that man of Greer's!" he exclaimed.

Yet as he said it, he became uncertain. Some other memory confused him, overlying this one with its shadowy image, as if he had exposed the same negative twice.

"Yes." Ginny drew away from him, opened her handbag and took out a comb. She dragged it through her furry short hair with quick, vicious strokes, as if she were punishing it for something. There was no expression on her face except perhaps a trace of apprehension. "I suppose he's been following us all day. And now he probably knows we know it. I'm afraid we overacted."

"Did you?" Colin asked.

She put her comb back in her bag, closed it and stood up.

"We were talking about John Clitheroe, d'you remember, whom you didn't think existed?" she said. "And about how my mother knew the picture had been stolen. And so on, and so on. Such a lot of things. And I asked you what you were going to do next about the picture and you haven't told me yet. But I'll tell you what I'm going to do."

"What?" Colin's mouth had become dry and his voice sounded harsh.

"I'm going back to Oldersfield."

"Now?"

"Yes."

"Ginny, don't." He reached for her hand. "Don't get some cock-eyed idea in your head you can steal the picture from Greer."

"There are other things to do besides that."

"Such as?"

"Talk to my mother. Find out if she knows Greer. Find out how she discovered the picture was valuable. Find out——" She was trying to keep the detachment of her tone, but on the last word her voice quavered. "—what else she's got herself involved in."

"Yes, I see."

"I've a lot of things to straighten out," she said.

"But you won't go near Greer yourself? Promise me that."

Her voice rose. "What's the point of a promise, Colin? I've broken plenty and I'll go on breaking them when I feel like it. I'm not a trustworthy character, you've guessed that yourself. So I'll do what I think best when I know what I'm up against. And you had better go back to Scotland."

"I was just going to say," Colin said evenly, as if he had not heard the note of hysteria in her voice, "it looks to me as if the next phase of the operation is in Scotland. We ought to find out what the aunts know about the picture and if Dickman's right that the law about market overt is quite different there. So why don't you come with me? "

" To Scotland? To Ardachoil? "

" Yes."

She gave a dry little laugh, yet her face had lit up.

" I'm afraid I haven't been invited," she said.

" I'm inviting you," said Colin.

" And that counts with the Lockie ladies, does it?"

" It had better."

" When are you going? "

" I thought, to-night. But if you've got to go back to Oldersfield for some luggage——"

" Oh, that wouldn't matter. But—no, Colin." The light died out of her face. " I think I'll just go back to Oldersfield. That'll be easiest for you, won't it? "

Sharply disappointed, he said, " Will you promise me not to go near Greer? "

" If that makes you feel any happier."

" Only you've just warned me you don't keep your promises."

" Some I do. But that one—well, it might be impractical."

He stood up and they started walking back towards the gates.

As they did so, the man in the raincoat, who had been resting on a bench a short distance away, stood up and came strolling after them.

CHAPTER EIGHT

SEEING THIS, Colin said urgently, "Ginny, come with me! We'll take the train to Edinburgh and pick up my car and drive on to Ardachoil."

"Because of that little man?" She laughed. "The right thing for us to do now is separate. It'll be interesting to find out which of us he's following."

"If you insist on going back to Oldersfield, I'm going too," Colin said.

"No, you're not. We're going to separate and you're going back to Scotland to find out who persuaded your aunts to have the picture cleaned, so that I can find out what connection that person has with my mother. And we'll both keep a watch over our shoulders to see which of us the little man's following."

"If it turns out he's following you, I'm going to follow him."

"No, don't. I don't want you to."

"I'm not always going to do exactly what you want, Ginny."

"But this time—please, Colin! You can't help me with my mother and she's what I've got to cope with when I get back. So please go home."

She spoke with such force that he hesitated. In that moment Ginny jumped into a passing taxi.

Twenty yards away the man in the raincoat paused, lit a cigarette and studied a clump of snowdrops until Colin started to walk slowly towards a bus stop. Then he came strolling after him.

Colin went to King's Cross. He had several hours to kill before the next train to Edinburgh, but he thought that he might as well go to the station and book a sleeper for the night.

The man in the raincoat travelled in the same bus with him. He got off at the same bus stop and followed Colin to the door of the Reservations office. He did not seem to care that Colin obviously knew that he was being followed.

Inside the office there was a queue of some length. Colin took his place at the end of it and as he moved slowly nearer to the counter, had time to think about what had happened.

Ginny had almost agreed to go to Ardachoil. She had wanted to go. Then suddenly she had decided against it and also that she did not want Colin in her way at Oldersfield. And because he had not quite believed that she meant it, had more than half expected some change in her mood and her plan, which would result in his having to go to Oldersfield with her whether he wanted to or not, he had let her get away. And now here he was, doing as she had told him, tamely setting off for Edinburgh with their shadow at his heels. . . .

But why had she arranged this? What was her real reason for it? Was it that she was not going back to Oldersfield at all?

If so, he realised, there was not much point in his asking himself where she was going instead. He knew too little about her to be able to make any guess at an answer. It would be more useful to stick to the assumption that she was returning to Oldersfield and then think out why it mattered to her if he came along too. Always supposing that she had not simply got tired of him, got bored, decided that one kiss was enough and that it was time to go back to her mother.

Colin had his wallet in his hand as he thought of this, and he was taking out some money in readiness to pay for his sleeper. He frowned at the notes, not really seeing them, but aware that they represented a necessity to make up his mind quickly about something or other.

Whether Ginny was returning to her mother or not, it didn't seem to matter to the man in the raincoat. It was what Colin was doing that he had been sent to find out, and perhaps, while he was at it, to try a little intimidation. Was this business of being shadowed supposed to impress on the young university lecturer that he was getting into deeper waters than he was used to?

A disturbing thing connected with that idea, Colin found, was that the thought of the man outside on the platform did stir a kind of fear in him. He had felt it when the man had walked past in Gray's Inn, leaving him with the confused conviction that this was not really Greer's manservant at all, but someone else, who meant something quite different in Colin's life.

But whoever he was, why be scared of him? What could he do in London's crowded streets, or the busy station? Pull out a gun? Throw a knife?

Deliberately crushing down that puzzling fear as he moved on a few steps in the queue to the counter, Colin started to think about Greer and what he was doing, alone in his fortress of a house at Hopewood. Actually Colin had no evidence that Greer lived there alone. He might have a wife, children, his aged parents and a host of servants living with him. But even when Colin had admitted this to himself, he went on feeling certain that Greer lived alone except for his one sinister manservant, the man with the pale, puffy face, the sly, vicious eyes, the thick eyebrows. . . .

A trickle of cold slid along Colin's nerves. They had been dark, the eyebrows of the man lying in the middle of the lonely Highland road, but that would have needed only a few strokes of a pencil. And if there was nothing that he could do here in King's Cross Station, there it had been easy. He had only had to lie and wait, while his accomplice hid in the bracken. His accomplice, Greer . . .?

" Yes, sir ? "

The clerk, whom Colin was now facing across the counter, was looking at him impatiently.

Hurriedly Colin pushed the notes back into his wallet and the wallet into his pocket.

" I'm sorry, I've just realised I've got mixed up," he said. " The wrong night. Sorry."

He strode away, aware that the clerk was shaking his head and muttering something about the sort of people who were allowed out loose, while several people in the queue started grinning.

In the doorway, seeing his shadow turning over the pages of a magazine at the bookstall, Colin paused and grinned too. Not a pleasant grin. Not one that many of his friends had ever seen on his face. After a moment he turned away and went to the cafeteria.

He knew that what he had to do now was keep his head, not give in to the fury that was pulsing through him. But as he worked his way along another queue to buy a cup of tea, he let himself dream of picking the man up by the throat, shaking him till his eyes bulged out of his head and throwing him on to the line as an engine came along to crush him flat. . . .

The man in the raincoat had come into the cafeteria a moment after him. He did not join in the queue between the counter and the railing. It would have been too easy for him to be trapped there if Colin had made a sudden dash for the door. Instead, sitting down with a grunt of weariness at a table between Colin and the nearest door, he lit a cigarette and opened an evening paper.

Colin did not look at him directly. He was afraid that his recognition, his recollection of that other meeting, would show too plainly on his face. He could feel his eyes giving him away, staring with an intensity that he could not control. The only thing to do with them was to fix them on his cup of tea. Perhaps in a little while he would let the man know that he had been recognised. On the other hand, perhaps not. He had to think that out.

Staring into his tea, stirring it mechanically, Colin wondered when the next train left for Oldersfield and what way there was of leaving the man behind here when he went to catch it. At first it seemed clear that he had to leave him behind. The air would be purer and his head clearer once he had shaken off the offensive presence. But after a few minutes he began to wonder if it would be worth the effort. Even if he managed to dodge away in the crowd, the man had merely to go to Charing Cross and look for him on the Oldersfield train.

In any case, he and Greer would soon know that Colin had returned to Oldersfield, for it was unlikely that Colin would be able to see Ginny without Harriet knowing of it and Harriet would tell Greer.

If Harriet was the link.

But of course she was the link.

Colin drank his tea, stood up in a leisurely way, went out and got into a taxi, noticing, as he had expected, that as it left the station on the way to Charing Cross, another taxi followed close behind it.

In the train to Oldersfield he again became absorbed in the thought of Ginny, and almost managed to stop caring about his shadow. It seemed to him now a matter of even greater importance than he had thought before to get her away from her mother. For if Harriet was the sort of woman who worked with men like Greer, something drastic had to be done. For Ginny to remain in that world would be both degrading and dangerous. Colin could not stand the thought of it.

Yet she might not see the situation just as he did. She had an anxious, protective loyalty to her mother and when she found out what Harriet was involved in, her main thought was likely to be how she could help to keep her out of trouble, failing to see that it was already too late to do that.

When the train reached Oldersfield, Colin saw his shadow ahead of him in the crowd at the barrier. But the man did not linger to make sure that Colin was going to the Green Tree Café. He went straight to a car that was parked in the station yard, got in and drove away. Colin found that it felt rather like being suddenly free of an unpleasant draught that had been blowing down his neck. It gave a lift to his spirits as he started the short walk to the market place. He passed Lake's saleroom, in which the lights were on although the doors were closed and in which he could see Beryl through the window, busy sorting and arranging. Reaching the café, he found it fairly full, with the two Heavens sisters trudging round among the tables with plates of beans on toast and cups of tea.

For some reason they looked flustered at seeing him and one of them managed to get in his way as he went to the door at the rear of the café.

" If it's Ginny you're looking for," she whispered to him, " she's come and gone."

" Gone? " he said helplessly. He had not been prepared for that.

" That's right."

" How long ago? "

" Couldn't say. We've been that busy. I didn't keep account of the time."

" Was it half an hour? An hour? "

" Five or ten minutes, more likely," said the old woman.

" Did she say where she was going? "

" Not a word."

" Or when she was coming back? "

" Not a word, just went running out. Maybe she'll be back again soon. She didn't say she wouldn't. If you'd like to sit down and wait——"

" What about Mrs. Winter? " Colin asked. " Is she in? "

Miss Heavens hesitated. " Well, she's in," she said reluctantly, " but she's a bit poorly. She wouldn't want to be disturbed."

" What's the matter with her? "

" Oh, there's nothing the *matter*. Just that she's taking it easy."

" I think I'll go down and see her then."

He took a step towards the door. The old woman moved swiftly to stand in his way again.

" Like I said, Mr. Lockie, she's resting, she doesn't want to be disturbed."

" I shan't disturb her for long."

He put a hand on Miss Heavens's shoulder, eased her aside, went through the door, across the kitchen and down the stairs to the basement.

" Mrs. Winter! " he called from halfway down. He did not want to scare Harriet by appearing without warning.

" Mrs. Winter," he said again outside her door, " it's me, Colin. Can I come in? "

He heard a muffled answer from inside. He did not know what it was, but he pushed the door open and went in.

For a moment, except for the red bars of the electric fire, the room seemed totally dark.

" It's all right, come on in, darling," Harriet said thickly from somewhere near the fire. " It's just that I don't want anyone to see me. I'm a hideous sight, simply hideous. I couldn't bear anyone looking at me when I'm like this."

He went towards her. As his eyes became used to the dark, he saw her sitting in a low chair by the fire, crouching down with a handkerchief covering most of her face. Her eyes, looking up at him over the top of the hankerchief, reflected the red light of the fire.

"You've been crying," he said, standing in front of her, feeling an immense embarrassment. He had not planned any interview with Harriet, particularly Harriet in the midst of an emotional storm. He only wanted to know where Ginny was.

"That's right, darling, crying my bloody eyes out," she answered with a sniff. "Well, wouldn't you? I came in, all upset already because I'd just heard of the death of a friend, a very old friend, almost my very oldest and dearest, and I found Ginny standing here. Standing here in the middle of the room, looking round as if she hated the place. And she could see I was upset—she always can—she always sees straight through me. And d'you know what she said to me? She said, 'I'm just going.' That's all. Literally, darling, that's all she said. And then she went." She gave a choking wail. "She was fond of him too, but she didn't even stop to hear about it. She's got a heart of stone."

"Do you know where she went?" Colin asked.

"I don't even know why she came," Harriet answered. "I don't know anything, except that everyone I care about dies. Yes, everyone. It isn't fair. And Ginny comes back and takes one look at me and says 'I'm just going,' as if— as if she didn't belong here—and then—then she just goes!"

Colin could see the gleam of a bottle and glass on the floor near Harriet's feet. He wondered if she had already done some drinking before she arrived home.

"Are you sure she really didn't say anything else?" he asked.

"Not a word, not a single, solitary, kind word! Could you have done that yourself, Colin? Could you have done it to a dog? Oh, she's my own daughter, I love her, but there are times when I could *kill* her, she hurts me so. I'd never be so unkind to anyone."

" I don't believe you would," he admitted.

"Not meaning it, anyway."

" Perhaps Ginny didn't mean it." He said it less to comfort Harriet than to defend Ginny, as if that had become his responsibility.

He saw her give her head a slight shake. Lowering the handkerchief from her face, she twisted it into a tight rope between her hands.

" I never know what she means," she said. " She's too complicated for me. I'm a simple sort of soul—a bit of a nitwit, I expect you think—but at least you know where you are with me. Don't you think so, Colin? Don't you think I'm really quite easy to get along with? "

" Of course you are."

He had not the heart to say anything else. But he said it with a sort of bewilderment, thinking that here was a woman who had connived at his being held up in his car, knocked out and left unconscious by the roadside, while her friends made off with a valuable picture that belonged to the women who had once befriended her and her daughter. And yet she was anxious to hear him say that she was easy to get along with.

And somehow she had made him feel that not to say it would have been shockingly brutal.

" Often I can't understand at all what gets into Ginny," she went on. " She'll be as sweet as anything for a little while and we'll have a wonderful time together—have real fun, you know—not doing anything special, but just laughing a lot at the same sort of things and enjoying ourselves. And then all of a sudden she's miles away. She's not in my world any longer. She might be on the other side of the moon. And I never know what I've said or done to make it happen and I don't know what to say or do to bring her back . . . . Whatever are you doing, Colin?"

He had stooped suddenly and was peering closely at her face. Even by the light of the fire he could see that there was more the matter with it than the ravages of tears.

As his hand went out to the switch of the table lamp near her, she gave a cry of protest and hid her face again, eyes and all, in the handkerchief.

" Put it out! " she cried. " I don't like it! "

Taking her hands in his, he gently forced them down from her face.

Down one side of it were long scratches with blood drying along them. There were smears of blood on her cheek and some more on the handkerchief.

" Who did that to you?" he asked.

" Nobody," she said. " I fell."

He shook his head. " Who was it? Tell me."

" Nobody! " She wrenched her hands away from him and covered her face again. " Why can't you put that bloody light out? "

He switched it off.

" Mrs. Winter, it wasn't Ginny . . .? "

She gave a shriek of laughter into her handkerchief. " God, that's funny! Ginny'll never use her nails on you, Colin. She'll use words—wicked, wicked words! And sometimes not even that, just blank, horrible silence."

" Who did use their nails on you, Mrs. Winter? "

" Nobody, I told you. I fell. I—I caught my heel in the cobbles out there and I fell."

" But Ginny saw it when you came in."

" No, she didn't. I had my handkerchief up over it. But I was crying. She could see I was crying and all she did was say, ' I'm just going,' and grab my handbag from me and

take my keys and go, as if—as if she couldn't care less
what had happened to me."

" Your keys—what keys? " Colin asked swiftly.

" The car keys, of course. She's always taking them."

" You didn't say anything about that before."

" Didn't I? I told you what she said, though. I told
you how all she said——"

He broke in, " So she's taken your car. Are you absolutely
certain she didn't say where she was going? "

" I keep telling you she didn't say a word."

" Well, I think I know. And I think I'd better go after
her as fast as I can."

She blew her nose, mopped at her eyes and gave a sigh.

" Well, I hope you find her. But listen—don't tell her
anything about my—my fall. You won't, will you? I
didn't really want her to stay and find out about it. I don't
want to worry her. It's just that I've never been any
good at standing up to things myself and yet I always
seem to have to do such a lot of it."

He gave her a touch on the shoulder. " You ought to
look after those scratches," he said. " Have you washed
them? "

" Been bathing them in my tears for the last half hour,
darling! "

" Disinfectant might be better."

" Oh, I don't know, tears are wonderful things," she
said. " They blot out time and every other damned thing.
Only it's bad to have someone looking on. Good-bye,
darling."

As Colin went to the door, she was reaching for the
bottle on the floor at her feet.

He went upstairs quickly. Going to the counter behind
which a Miss Heavens was filling cups of tea from a tea
urn, he asked, " D'you know if there's a car-hire place
anywhere near here? "

" Just across the square," she said, " the other side of the car park. Was she still . . .? I mean, is she all right? "

" I'm not quite sure," he answered. " Is she often like this? "

" Well, she's one of those who's up one minute, down the next," said the old woman. " She may be bright as a bird to-morrow."

" Then it may be nothing much. All the same, she seems to have hurt herself. A fall, she says. It might be a good idea to look in on her presently."

" Reckon I could do that."

" Thanks."

He crossed the café to the door, went out and walked quickly across the quiet market place, between the empty stalls, to the garage beyond the car park.

He found the man in charge and said that he wanted a car to take him to Hopewood. The man said it could be managed, disappeared into the office and came out again, putting a greasy blue chauffeur's cap on his head. Calling out to an invisible figure at the back of the garage. to take over, he went to a very old Rolls that was standing at the kerb and got into the driver's seat.

As they started off, Colin took out his wallet, went through his pockets and carefully counted his money. It was lucky, he thought, that he had decided against paying for that sleeper to Edinburgh. It was lucky also that the Royal Society made a habit of paying your travelling expenses on the spot. All the same, he was getting uncomfortably low. He would have to see about getting someone to cash a cheque next day. And if for some reason he did not seeing himself getting back to Edinburgh to-morrow, it would be as well to telephone the department and do a little explaining, or he might find himself becoming unpopular in certain quarters.

Not that he had the faintest idea how to explain what

had been happening. Could he call it family trouble? Say that he had had to have legal advice?

His mind clung to the relatively minor problem as the car carried him through the lamplit outskirts of the town and out on to the dark highway.

He had a faint hope he might have been wrong when he guessed that Ginny had borrowed her mother's car to take her to Hopewood. But as the old Rolls circled the village green and took the turning that led past the wall of Greer's garden, he saw the red Mini-Minor driven off the road on to the grass verge about twenty yards from the big wrought iron gates. It looked as if Ginny had left it there so that her arrival should not be seen from the house.

" Want me to wait for you? " the driver of the hired car asked as Colin got out and paid him.

" No thanks," Colin said. " I think I can get a lift back."

" Good-night then."

" Good-night."

The car drove off.

When it had gone, its lights disappearing round the bend in the road, Colin suddenly became aware that the night was very black and wild. The sky was covered with low, scurrying cloud. A wind with a sting of rain in it made the tree-tops fret and mutter.

Standing at the gate, he could not see the lights of the village and the only light from the house came dimly through a chink in the heavy curtains that covered the windows of Greer's drawing-room, the room where the Decayed Gentlewoman hung. The garden, with its high, enclosing wall, was a pit of shadow.

Colin put out a hand to one of the heavy gates to push it open.

Just then a light shone out down the drive. Someone had

thrown open the door of the house. As he stood still, he saw a slight figure, awkwardly carrying something, appear for an instant in the doorway, then the door swung shut again. The garden returned to darkness.

But stumbling uneven footsteps were hurrying over the gravel towards him. Carrying the picture, holding it before her like a shield, Ginny was almost upon him before she saw him. She gave a gasp of fear, then gasped, " Colin! Thank God it's you! Here—you take this and let's get out of here fast."

CHAPTER NINE

She went running towards the little red car before Colin had had time to answer.

Not that he had anything to say just then. For a moment he remained staring at the house, expecting to see the door burst open again, to hear shouts and pounding footsteps. But the dark front of the house remained as it was. Only the one chink of light showed between the curtains of the upstairs room, like a mocking little smile on an otherwise expressionless face.

The darkness and emptiness of the place sent a chill through him. He swung away from the gate and went running after Ginny.

She was tumbling into the driving seat. He heard her quick, sobbing breath as she leant across the car, pushed the farther door open, tipped forward the seat beside her and helped him to slide the picture on to a pile of rugs and coats in the back of the car.

As soon as he was in it himself, before he had even slammed the door shut, she sent it bouncing off the verge into the road and back towards the village.

Colin waited until they had circled the green and shot out on to the main road before he said, " Ginny, what in God's name——? "

" Don't ! " she cried in a high-pitched voice. " Don't talk to me ! "

" But I've got to know—— "

" Wait ! I'll tell you all about it presently. I can't now. I just can't talk or think. Wait a little."

He slid down lower in his seat, looking at the pallor of her face, then at the road ahead.

She was driving too fast. The rain was growing heavier and the road was greasy. He could feel the car swerve and skid as she took a corner. He thought of suggesting that he should take over the driving, but guessed that nothing would make her stop yet to change places.

Near the crest of a small hill she had to jam on the brakes, because she had been trying to pass a lorry when another car, appearing over the hill, came bearing down on them. The other car braked, swerved almost into the ditch and passed with the driver mouthing curses at her.

" Sorry," she said to Colin, whose head had almost hit the windscreen. " Sorry, that was bad."

After that she was more careful, but the way that she crouched over the wheel and the tension of her jaw told Colin that it was not yet time to start talking.

Suddenly she left the Oldersfield road, taking a sharp turning to the left into a narrow road with a bad surface and high hedges on both sides.

He asked, " Where does this take us? "

" It's a short cut on to the A22," she answered.

" And where does that go? "

" Croydon."

" Why are we going to Croydon? "

" Because I think the easiest way to get on to the A1

from here is to go slap though London. Don't worry, I know the way."

"That's fine," said Colin, "even if that little matter is quite the least of my worries. But just in case you're heading for Scotland, Ginny, I'm almost sure we have an extradition treaty with the English."

"Don't!" she cried again. "Please don't *talk* to me. I'll tell you everything as soon as I can—Oh God!" She jammed the brakes on again. "I'm sorry, I think I'm going to be sick."

She flung open the door, plunged across the road and disappeared through the hedge.

It was several minutes before she reappeared. When she did, she came back to the car with dragging feet. Her mad need for speed had gone.

"Shall I drive for a bit now?" Colin suggested. "You can take over again when we get to London."

She drew a shaky breath. "Would you? I'm awfully sorry about this. I've a terribly nervous stomach. It gets upset at the least bit of excitement."

She walked round to the other side of the car as Colin changed seats inside.

"Actually I feel better now," she said as they started again. "Things don't seem quite so swimmy."

"Good, then perhaps you'll feel like doing this talking you promised," he said. "We seem to have shed the pursuit, so you needn't worry about that any more."

"There wasn't any pursuit," she answered. "I knew there wouldn't be, I wasn't worrying about that."

"You *knew* there wouldn't be any . . .?" Something heaved uncomfortably inside Colin, though he was not sure what he feared.

"There wasn't anyone there," Ginny explained. "The house was empty. So they don't know we've got the thing yet."

"I see. The house was empty. You walked in, walked out again. Simple. Why all the hurry then?"

He was keeping his eyes on the road, but he was aware that she turned her head to give him a long look.

"The house *was* empty," she said. "And I did walk in and walk out again. And I was in a hurry because I felt so awful. I nearly passed out with terror. You may not believe me, but this is positively my first burglary."

"I thought," he said, "you'd probably claim it wasn't a burglary."

"Well, it wasn't, of course, in a technical sense. I was simply acting as your agent, recovering what I honestly believe to be your property."

"A self-appointed agent," he said grimly.

"Anyhow, I know it felt just like a burglary," she said. "Quite an ordinary burglary. It wasn't too bad till I actually got the picture down from the wall, but from the moment I did that I felt certain I was going to walk into Greer and that he'd instantly be dialling 999 and screaming blue murder."

"He might have done something worse than that," said Colin.

She did not answer.

"Didn't you see him at all?" he asked.

"No."

"Nor that man of his?"

"No."

"I don't understand it."

"Well, the man was in London, wasn't he?"

"No, I'm afraid he wasn't," Colin said. "He followed me to Oldersfield, then dropped me at the station, got into a car and drove off. I assumed he was going to Hopewood."

"What I don't understand," she said, "is how you ever

got to Hopewood yourself. I thought you were going back to Edinburgh."

" I'll tell you about that presently. Tell me the rest of your burglary story. How did you get into the house? "

" I just walked in. The door wasn't locked."

" You walked straight in without even looking round beforehand? "

" Oh, I rang up first. You see, it suddenly struck me when I saw the man following us in London that perhaps— just perhaps—the house in Hopewood might be empty. After all, Greer must go out sometimes, mustn't he? So as soon as I got back to the café, I telephoned and there wasn't any answer. I waited a little while, then I tried again. I let the bell ring for ages and there still wasn't any answer. As it happened, I had to wait a bit longer then, because I needed the car keys and unluckily Mother was out, but she came in quite soon and I got the keys from her and took the car and left."

" I saw your mother," Colin said.

" Did you? Then I suppose she told you all that. Well, I drove over to Hopewood. I hadn't really any plan, except that if the house was empty, I was going to have a shot at getting in. To be on the safe side, I rang up once more from the call-box in the village and again didn't get any answer. So then I went ahead. I left the car a little way from the gates and went in. But then I had a shock, because there were lights on in the house. There were lights in that upstairs room, where the picture was, and there was light coming out at the front door."

" You mean the door was open? " Colin said.

" Yes. Only a little way open. All the same, I could see light round the edge of it. It blazed at me all the way from the gate. I didn't know what to make of it. So I rang the bell. Actually I rang several times and then I knocked and then I called. And there wasn't a sound inside the place. So I thought Greer must be one of those people who leave lights on in a house, whenever they go out, to keep burglars away, and I went in. I went on calling all the way up the stairs, ' Mr. Greer, Mr. Greer! '—because I'd some idea that if he did suddenly pounce out on me from somewhere, he couldn't possibly say I was breaking and entering, or whatever it was I was really doing, so long as I was making enough noise about it. And as I told you, it didn't feel too bad until I'd got the picture down from the wall. But after that, if he'd come in, I don't know what I could have said. So I just ran for it. And I've never in my life been as frightened as I was during those few moments. And then seeing someone at the gate . . . ! " She gave a shudder at the memory. " Realising it was you was one of the most wonderful moments of my life."

" I was quite glad to see you too," Colin said dryly. " But there's something very peculiar about this story of yours, Ginny."

" It's true, every word of it," she said quickly.

" I still don't understand it and I don't like it. That open door. . . . Who left it open and why? "

" Don't you think it was just an accident? Someone thought they'd shut it, but the latch hadn't quite caught."

" That doesn't sound to me the sort of accident that would ever happen to Greer. And what about the other man? Where's he got to? If he drove to Hopewood when he dropped me at the station, he'd have got there long before I did—before you did too."

" He could have got there, found Greer was out and decided to go to the pub. He could have been the one who left the door open."

" If either of those two left the door open, it was intentional," Colin said. " They wanted you—or someone—to do just what you did."

" They couldn't have wanted that."

" I admit I can't see why they should."

" So what you mean is, you don't believe me. You don't believe the door was open at all. You probably think I'm in cahoots with those two in some mysterious scheme to do you down. Perhaps you even think I'd a key to the door and could come and go as I liked."

They had just reached the turning into the main road. Colin was concentrating on the traffic streaming past, waiting for the moment when he could cut across it. The rain was falling heavily now and he had had to set the windscreen wipers going. As they rocked backwards and forwards against the dazzle of the lights flashing by, his eyes had narrowed and his forehead set into a hard frown.

" You don't believe me," Ginny repeated softly.

He sent the car forward and turned it towards London.

" Ginny, your mother told me you took her keys," he said. " I asked her what keys and she said her car keys. But was that really all? She was very angry with you, very upset. It wasn't because you'd found the key to Greer's house in her handbag, was it? "

" No," she answered with a sigh, " that was for a quite simple reason. She wanted me to stay with her. She always wants me to stay with her. And the trouble is I—I can't bear very much of it. If you think that's heartless, I can't help it. Something in me goes completely to pieces if I see too much of her. And yet I love her. . . . No, I only took the car keys."

" Did you know she'd been hurt? "

" *Hurt?*"

" Yes," Colin said, " she said she'd had a fall. It looked to me more as if someone had raked their nails down the side of her face. Could that have been her dear friend Beryl? "

"Oh God!" She was staring at him. "No, I didn't see. . . . But I remember she had her handkerchief to her face when she came in. And she was crying."

"Did she tell you about a friend who'd died?"

"No. What friend?"

"She didn't say who it was. But she said you were fond of him too."

"I—I don't know who it could be," she said. "It just might not be anybody. I mean, sometimes it's really all in the past. My father. Harry Winter. Colin, do you think we ought to turn back?"

"I don't think she was badly hurt, if that's what you mean."

"Are you sure?"

"About that, yes. But listen, Ginny, I'm also sure she's deep in with Greer over this picture affair and that she must have been from the start. So I'm not too happy about saying she's all right. It's something I think we ought to talk over before we go much farther with what we're doing now."

She let her head droop, resting it on her hand.

"I've been getting more and more afraid of it," she said listlessly, "although in a way I can't really believe it. Because she isn't like that. I mean, she isn't calculating or greedy. Quite the reverse. I'm a monster of avarice compared with her."

"Suppose she'd fallen in love with a calculating, greedy man, or suppose Greer used her without her quite understanding how," Colin suggested.

"I suppose that could happen."

"I'll tell you something I found out this afternoon, Ginny. Greer and that man of his are the people who held me up on the road from Ardachoil."

She lifted her head quickly. "How do you know?"

" I suddenly recognised the man, that's all. I couldn't possibly prove it. All the same, it's something I'm quite sure of."

" And you think Mother's the person who told them about the picture? "

" I don't know," he admitted. " She isn't a person who knows about pictures, is she? "

Ginny gave a short laugh. "No."

" And she hasn't been to Ardachoil or seen any of the aunts for years."

" No."

" So I can't really understand where she fits in. Yet she has to be the link somehow, or the coincidence of the two of you being on the spot where the sale was to happen is a bit too much to swallow."

" That sale," Ginny said, " in market overt—it was all arranged, wasn't it? "

" As I see it," Colin replied, " what happened was this. Greer somehow or other discovered the value of the picture. Let's skip just how he did it and what it is. The aunts may know something that'll help to clear that up. Anyway, he somehow organised things so that they were persuaded to send it to Edinburgh to be cleaned. And he knew just when I was going to take it and he lay in wait for me and stole it. Then he had the strength of mind to do nothing for over two years. I suppose he was waiting all the time for the right opportunity to crop up. And the right opportunity was Mrs. Sibbald, an old woman living alone in a houseful of junk that was going to be sold off cheap at the local saleroom by your friend Joe Lake."

Ginny opened her mouth to say something, then closed it again, pressing her lips tightly together.

Colin went on, " Think how simple it must have been for the Lakes to add the picture to one of the lots in the saleroom and say it came from Mrs. Sibbald's attic. It need never have been in the house at all. Her nephew wouldn't have known if it had been or not. Then all they had to do was have it on show for a few days where the public could get in to see it and then sell it to Greer at their regular Thursday auction. And that would be a perfect sale in market overt. The picture would become legally Greer's and he could go ahead very innocently having it examined by experts and recognised for whatever it really is. Then he could put it up for sale at Sotheby's and get some enormous price for it, much higher than if he'd sold it under the counter to some shady collector. I think that was the whole object of the plan—to be able to sell it again quite openly and get the sort of price valuable pictures do fetch nowadays."

Ginny frowned at the rainwashed windscreen and the dully gleaming wet road.

"If you're right, d'you realise something, Colin?—the picture must be simply terrifically valuable. I mean, for all this scheming to have been worth while."

"I know," he said.

"And there it hung all those years at Ardachoil, nobody knowing a thing about it!"

"And there it hung this evening in Greer's house, quite a lot of people knowing *all* about it," he said, "and yet the door was open."

"Yes, I see that's odd," said Ginny.

A little while later she took over the driving again. She knew the labyrinth of London as well as she knew the lanes around Oldersfield. From time to time Colin looked out through the rear window, thinking that the lights of some particular car were remaining close to them suspiciously long, but each time the car sooner or later turned off the road behind them, or overtook them and vanished ahead.

Ginny told him again not to worry about pursuit.

" But the sooner we get to Ardachoil the better," she said. " Once your aunts have the picture back I don't see what Greer can really do about it, quite apart from the law about market overt being different there. Don't you agree? "

As Colin did not answer at once, she repeated, " Don't you agree? Possession, I mean, being nine points of the law."

" I was just wondering," he said, " why you're so keen the aunts should have the picture back."

" Why shouldn't I ? " she said. " It's theirs."

" But I've gathered that you aren't exactly fond of them."

" What's that got to do with it? Anyway, I may be fonder than I sound. I'll tell you more about that sometime."

" I wish you could tell me more about Greer's house," he said. " That open door . . ."

It worried him more than anything else that had happened that evening, unless it was the problem of what had become of the man who had followed them about London in the afternoon. Where had he gone from the station if he hadn't gone to Hopewood? Had he gone to see the Lakes? Had Greer been waiting for him there? Had there been a meeting of the conspirators in the office behind the saleroom, from which Harriet for some reason, such as a sudden row blowing up between her and Beryl, had been sent away?

That might be the real explanation of Harriet's tears and the scratches on her face. But it didn't explain the open door.

Ginny went on driving until they had left Stevenage behind and they decided to stop for a meal. They stopped at a lorry drivers' café and had fish and chips, thick bread and butter and tea. Afraid of leaving the picture in the car, they took it into the café with them and propped it against the leg of their table. From time to time they took puzzled looks at the faded face, shadowed by the plumed hat, the pearl ear-rings, the folded hands.

"Don't you really know anything about her?" Ginny asked. "Haven't you any family legends about some ancestor around that time, a Royalist or a Roundhead, whichever you're lot were?"

He shook his head. "I can trace my family back reliably to my four grandparents and I know a certain amount about two or three of my great-grandparents and there I stick."

"I like legends," Ginny said dreamily. "There's the one I grew up on about Mother's childhood. Everyone was beautiful, everyone was kind, everyone was rich. And generous too, which must have been so pleasant. Actually her father was rector in a Somerset village and he can't have been as kind and generous as all that, or we'd have seen a bit more of him. I can just remember him coming to visit us once in London, a fat solemn little man who sat there shaking his head and muttering to himself, then suddenly he pushed a bag of sweets into my hand and got up and bolted. I think it stuck in my mind chiefly because Mother had one of her crying spells after it, which went on for the rest of the day."

"Didn't he ever come again?" Colin asked.

"Not that I remember. But there must have been just a little truth in her view of what things were like once upon a time because she's gone on expecting the same pattern to be repeated wherever else she's been. And the odd thing is, she keeps finding it. Take your aunts. Whatever had she in common with any of them? And yet they practically gave her and me a second home for all those years. No, not a second home—our only one, really, because when we weren't there we were nearly always on the move. Mother would go for a year or so as a housekeeper to someone who didn't mind having a child along with her. Then she'd have a spell in an office, either having a love-affair with her boss or getting bored because there wasn't a chance of one. Then she had a spell of trying to get on to the stage, but that didn't last very long. Really the only thing that lasted was Ardachoil. . . ."

She picked up her teacup. Folding her hands round it and putting her elbows on the table, she went on in a sub-dued voice, " The queer thing is, you know, I could have sworn Mother was really grateful for that. I could have sworn she really loved those women, even if she was hurt and offended when they didn't want us any more. I thought she understood they'd done something for me that's made an enormous difference to the whole of my life and I thought that was the sort of thing she'd remember. And yet she went and did—this to them! " She gestured at the picture propped against the table leg.

" So that's why you're working so hard to see the Decayed Gentlewoman home again," Colin said.

" Yes, of course. I can't stand what I've found out in the last few days, so first the picture's going back and then I—I'll try to sort things out at home, find out what really happened, what Mother's mixed up in and if I can get her out of it, and then I . . ." She frowned and did not finish the sentence. Looking at her empty tea cup, she said, " I think I want some more tea."

Colin looked round, failed to catch the eye of the waitress, turned back to Ginny and said, " If I were you, I shouldn't go back."

" Wouldn't you? "

" No."

" You would," she said.

" Don't go, Ginny," I said. " Keep out of it. Please."

" Why? "

" You've upset their plans and they're dangerous people."

" But while Mother's there——"

" Stop worrying about your mother, Lead your own life."

" Oh, Colin, darling——"

" And don't call me darling ! "

" No, I know I shouldn't," she agreed. " Yet I suppose it's a word that meant something once—something worth saying. It's a pity, the way such a lot of things get spoilt. I was going to say. . . ." Her hand touched his, then she drew it away. " I forget what I was going to say. And I don't think I want any more tea after all. Shall we get on? "

She led the way to the door.

Driving on northwards, they found less traffic on the road and presently the rain stopped and a watery moon appeared between the clouds. The tree tops were dark and still. With Colin driving again, Ginny soon fell asleep, or if not quite asleep, at least into a silent stupor of fatigue, lolling in her seat, propping her head with her arm.

They made good time through Huntingdon, Grantham, Doncaster. At Scotch Corner Colin took the road to the west, making for Glasgow. It was early morning when they crossed the Border.

CHAPTER TEN

THEY SAW THE REMAINS of snow on the hills. It lay here
and there in gleaming patches on the blackish brown of the
dry heather, touched with a rosy sparkle by the early
sunshine. The sky was blue and clear. But when Ginny
and Colin got out of the car to have a quick cup of tea,
cold stung their faces. It made Ginny jerk the collar of her
sheepskin jacket up round her ears. She was still very
pale and there were violet smudges under her eyes, but she
had lost the look of extreme tension that she had had all
the evening before. She seemed to feel that the worst of
the job was over.

Colin was not at all sure of this.

They waited until they reached Glasgow to have a real
breakfast, then made it a slow and splendid affair in a hotel,
with fruit juice, porridge, bacon and eggs, large quantities of
toast and marmalade and an extra pot of coffee. Even so,
when they had finished, Colin felt that he could easily go
through the meal all over again. After breakfast Ginny
said that she must do some shopping and disappeared into a
Marks and Spencer's. While she was gone, Colin walked
up and down to stretch his legs after the night's driving,
but always stayed near enough to the car to keep an eye
on the picture.

He tried to think of a suitable story to tell when they got
to Ardachoil. He knew that it would have to be a long and
detailed story. The aunts liked details. They liked exact-
ness. They liked as little as possible left to the imagination.
Imagination, after all, was not their strong point. Colin
smiled, thinking of them with amused but deep affection.
He was really far more attached to them than he was to his

parents, who were pleasant, much travelled people, with whom he was on very good terms, but who had nearly always been too far away to be quite real to him. Even now they were far away. After most of a lifetime in the tropics, the climate of the British Isles had not recommended itself to them and they had settled, on his father's retirement, in Jamaica.

Walking up and down, he tried to decide how much to tell the aunts about Ginny's mother. For Ginny's sake, he wanted to say as little as possible. Yet he had to find out from them what their quarrel with Harriet had been about and how, in spite of her not having been to see them for years, she had known that the picture was to be taken to Edinburgh. He had to know through whom she had been receiving her news of what was happening at Ardachoil.

For a moment he wondered if it was conceivable that it was one of the aunts themselves. But that was so totally unlikely that he grinned. It would have had to be all three of them or none. They always acted together in almost uncanny harmony.

Ginny appeared just then at his elbow. She had stowed her parcels into a new plastic zip-bag.

" Do you know you've a rather sinister smile, Colin? " she said. " Most of the time you look so easy-going and good tempered and then one catches sight of you when you've forgotten one's around and one thinks, ' My God, what's really going on inside him? ' "

He laughed as they got into the car.

" I hadn't a sinister thought in my head," he said.

"That's all the worse. It means you don't even know what's going on there and it'll come bursting out one day when you least expect it."

They had about another hundred miles to go. Ginny drove again for a time through Dumbarton and Helensburgh and northwards up the side of Loch Long. But beyond Arrochar, where the higher mountains came closer, she told Colin that she could not keep her eyes off them and that he had better take over again.

As he drove on, she treated him to an exclamatory travelogue of wonder at the rich sunny blue of Loch Fyne with the silver slopes of snow beyond it, the glitter of some thread of water weaving down over black rock, the massed daffodils in cottage gardens.

" I needn't remind you," Colin said when she asked with a sigh why one ever went abroad, " that the weather isn't always like this."

" But when it is, is there anywhere in the world like it? "

" Probably not."

They passed Inverary and Lochgilphead and continued north along the main road to Oban, with a sea of glittering blue on their left. It was mid-afternoon when the car reached the turning that led to Ardachoil. Five minutes before that they had come to the spot where Colin had been held up. He had pointed it out to Ginny.

" Well, if you see a body lying in the middle of the road this time," she said, " mind you drive slap over it and keep on going."

Colin gave the little grin that Ginny had called sinister. He did not admit to her that for a few miles before they reached the place he had been uneasily on the alert, unnaturally watchful of any car that passed, or anyone standing by the roadside. Even the sudden rising of a lapwing out of the heather made his muscles tense. He was not, of course, expecting a repetition of what had happened before. In fact, he did not know what he was expecting. Just trouble of some kind. Sometime. Somewhere.

The side road was only wide enough for one car, had a rough, sandy surface, pitted with holes, and was only a few feet above the level of the small sea-loch that it skirted.

They had gone about a quarter of a mile along this road when Ginny gave a cry, " Oh look—the palm trees! "

And there they were, familiar enough to Colin for him to have driven past without thinking about them, yet really looking utterly improbable on either side of the garden gate of one of the small houses that more or less adhered to the village of Ardachoil.

" They look a bit sad and exhausted, don't they? " Ginny went on. " As if they've never truly got over the journey."

" Still they're alive and growing," Colin said.

" You don't know the trouble they've got me into one time and another," she said with a laugh. " I used to tell the girls at school that palm trees grew in the Highlands and they wrote me off as a liar straight away. I *was* rather a liar, of course, about lots of things. Colin——" Her voice wavered.

He manœuvred the car round a pot hole in the middle of the road and on past a great thicket of rhododendrons.

" Yes? " He saw that the evergreen of the bushes was flecked with the red of the opening buds and that on the hillside above them the silver birches were wrapped in a soft haze of new green.

" I think I'm beginning to get nervous," Ginny said.

" There's no need," he reassured her. " The aunts will behave themselves. They've got very rigid standards of courtesy."

" I'm terrified of courtesy. And what are we going to say about how we got hold of—her? " She jerked a thumb at the back of the car.

" Leave it to the inspiration of the moment."

" Your inspiration or mine?"

" Mine," he said quickly.

" All right."

The car climbed successfully out of another hole in the

road and slithered through a drift of sand at a bend. Ahead was a small ivy-grown church, a post-office, a red telephone box and the Lockies' white house.

Ginny bit her thumb and stared straight ahead of her as Colin drove in at the gate. The car had been seen from the windows of the house. By the time that Colin had unfolded himself from the driving seat, the front door had been thrown open and one aunt after another came bursting out, like a row of soap bubbles out of a pipe.

First came Dolly, then Phyllis, and then, a little more slowly and stiffly than her sisters, Clara, who was nearly seventy and at last, Colin thought as he went to meet them, beginning to show it.

They were all tall, bony women, with curly white hair, bright blue eyes and ruddy, weather-beaten faces. They all wore tweed skirts which had been hand-woven by Dolly, and made up by Phyllis. Their twin-sets had been knitted by Clara, as always in the favourite colour of each, blue for Clara, green for Phyllis, pink for Dolly. They all wore a number of brooches and lockets and bracelets, inherited from their mother.

"Colin!" cried Dolly as he embraced her. "This *is* a wonderful surprise! The last person we were expecting——"

"—to see," said Phyllis. "When we heard the car and looked out——"

"—we said, 'That can't be Colin,'" said Clara, "'it's not his car.'"

"But I thought to myself—" said Dolly.

"—he could buy a new car," said Phyllis.

"As it seems you have," said Clara.

All three stood looking at the car with tentative smiles of welcome on their kind, beaming faces, waiting for Colin to introduce the friend who remained inside it.

He went back to the car and opened the door.

"Come on out," he said. "They aren't going to eat you."

Ginny got out and walked towards the three Lockie ladies. They advanced a little way to meet her, but waited for the magic words of introduction to make it safe for them to show their great pleasure in the unexpected visit of a stranger.

They always loved to meet strangers in this remote place, but they were all very shy women, who clung to certain rules of behaviour, as to a stout rope, that would save them, non-swimmers that they were, from floundering out of their depths among the mysterious currents of human relationships.

"Don't you recognise her?" Colin asked, putting an arm round Ginny's shoulders and drawing her forward.

"*Recognise* her?" said Dolly. "We ought to *recognise* her?"

It was a challenge. All the aunts had long memories.

It was their pride that they never forgot a face, or a name to attach to the face, or anything else important about anyone whom they had ever known, down to how many lumps of sugar they liked in their tea.

"You've taken us so completely by surprise," Dolly went on. "But it's a fact I had a feeling as soon as I saw her . . ."

"I believe we all had a feeling . . ." said Phyllis.

"That we knew her very well," said Clara.

"And if you'll just give us a moment . . ." said Dolly. "Why, yes, of course——!"

"Of course we know!" cried Phyllis.

"It's little Ginny Jerrold," said Clara and held her arms out.

"My dear," she went on a moment later, with Ginny hugging her, "you must forgive us for not recognising you at once, but you've changed considerably since we saw you last."

"Far more than we have ourselves," said Phyllis.

"Dear me, yes," said Dolly. Her eyes suddenly misted with tears. "You were just a wee bit of a girl and we were already old women. Or no doubt you would think so. It's so long ago, perhaps we weren't really so old. But we're very glad to see you after all this time."

"We're all glad," said Phyllis.

"You've arrived just in time for tea," said Clara.

She led the way into the house.

As Phyllis followed her and Ginny was taken into the house by Dolly, who had put an arm through hers and seemed to cling to her, Colin went to the car, took out the picture and carried it into the sitting-room, where the aunts and Ginny had gathered round the fire.

It was a small room, packed tight with furniture that had come from a much larger house, but was all too much beloved to be thinned out for the mere sake of convenience. The windows looked out on the hillside covered with the daffodils that Ginny had remembered at jonquils.

Exclamations of amazed delight came from the aunts when they saw the picture.

"But this is one of the great days of our lives," said Dolly. "And to think that when we got up this morning we never knew——"

"——anything at all unusual was going to happen!" cried Phyllis.

"To-day is Tuesday," said Clara. "The butcher calls on Tuesday, but that's all that happens."

"The Decayed Gentlewoman!" Dolly gave a happy laugh. "Do you children remember how you used to call her that? We couldn't think whom you were referring to so rudely."

"Unless indeed it was one of ourselves," said Phyllis.

"Only why one of us, more than another?" said Clara. "So it hardly seemed to fit. Colin must hang the picture up for us after tea."

"Where did you find it after all this time?" Dolly asked.

Colin brought out the answer to this that he had prepared.

"Ginny saw it in a saleroom and recognised it. She got in touch with me—I was in London at the time—and we managed to get it back."

"You bought it, Ginny?" said Dolly. "How kind, very kind!"

"We've always missed it so," said Phyllis.

"You must tell us what you had to pay for it," said Clara.

"Of course," said Dolly. "We must pay you back."

"At once," said Phyllis.

"Oh, it was nothing," Ginny told them, avoiding Colin's eye. "Really nothing."

"But we insist—" the three sisters began together.

"I won't hear of it," Ginny said firmly. "Truly, it was nothing at all."

Saying that they would not argue the matter now, but would return to it later, which Colin knew they most certainly would, Dolly went out to lay the tea table and make the tea.

This was always done by Dolly, as the scones and cakes were always baked by Phyllis and the table presided over by Clara. In their life together, the aunts had long ago arranged a certain division of labour and each clung jealously to her own duties, only demanding of the other two that they should frequently express their admiration of the skill and devotion with which she performed her tasks.

As soon as Dolly was gone, Phyllis said to Ginny that

she was sure that she would like a wash and bore her away to the bathroom. This left Colin alone with his eldest aunt, a situation which he had known would be brought about pretty quickly. For he could see that the aunts were boiling over with questions which they were too polite to ask in front of Ginny, and the asking of questions, the getting to the bottom of things, was Clara's department.

" Well, Aunt Clara," he said with a smile as she sat down in a high-backed tapestry armchair near the fire and rested her long, thin feet on the fender, "what do you want me to tell you first?"

"What do you suppose?" she asked.

"Are Ginny and I engaged to be married?" he suggested. "No, we aren't, dearest Aunt Clara."

"Now, Colin, as if I would pry into your private affairs before you were ready to tell me of them of your own accord," she said. "No, all I want is the truth about your discovery of this picture."

"What we told you was the truth."

"I hope so. But my impression is it was not the whole truth."

"The whole truth is an awfully long and complicated story," he said. "I can't possibly get it in before tea."

"Very well then, you and I will go for a walk afterwards and you will tell it to me then."

"Nothing could suit me better. There are a few things I want you to tell me too, Aunt Clara."

"Apart from that, she appears a nice girl, Colin."

"I'm glad you think so."

"But I can't have Dolly upset. That woman, her mother, was Dolly's friend. It wouldn't surprise me if poor Dolly still remembers her with affection, in spite of everything. She has a very affectionate heart."

"I know she has," Colin said. "What I don't understand is what Ginny's mother did that was so terrible."

Clara gave him a thoughtful glance. "Is that a fact, Colin?"

"Of course, she wasn't married," he said, having decided to get this over to his aunt with the greatest possible casualness, "but that was only because Ginny's father couldn't get a divorce."

"Tt, tt, as if we didn't know that from the first," Clara said. "It made us sorry for her and even more so for the child."

"Then what did she do?"

Clara reached out a hand to pat his. "We'll take a walk together after tea, Colin. My story may be as long and complicated as yours. Meanwhile, not a word."

"Not a word, Aunt Clara."

They had tea in the dining-room, as they always did, a substantial meal at which a little of everything had to be tried, or Aunt Phyllis's feelings would have been hurt. Afterwards Colin hung the picture in its old place, where it could hardly be seen because of the shadow cast by the massive, carved sideboard. But the aunts all claimed to recognise signs of positive satisfaction on the dim face of the unknown lady at having come safely back to her old home. They thanked Ginny and Colin again and again.

Then Phyllis and Dolly started to clear the table and when Ginny offered to help with the washing up, the offer was eagerly accepted, while Clara said that in the circumstances she and Colin would only be in the way in the kitchen and would go for a short walk. Colin could have sworn that the aunts had had no chance to discuss the making of this arrangement, yet each had known what was required of her. He sometimes thought that this smooth, wordless co-operation must seem a slightly frightening thing to strangers, but he was so used to it himself that he accepted it as part of the natural order of things.

Clara put on her boots and a tweed coat that she had

had for as long as Colin could remember and together they walked on along the steadily deteriorating road towards the sea. The sun was going down in copper flames behind the Paps of Jura. A purple haze joined the sky and the sea. The islands had become dark shapes of mystery and were slowly vanishing away into the engulfing shadows.

The road ended at a small ruined croft. Beyond it a rough track led across boggy ground, then up on to the cliffs. Clara took Colin's arm. They walked slowly, sometimes pausing to look at the deepening colours of the sunset.

"To answer your question, Colin," Clara said, "why we stopped making Harriet Jerrold welcome at Ardachoil—I don't suppose you ever knew, did you, that Dolly was once engaged to be married?"

"Engaged?" Colin said in astonishment. "Aunt Dolly?"

He had to restrain an impulse to say that it would surely be impossible for any man to marry only one of the aunts. He would have to marry all three of them together.

Clara gave a rather cold smile. "Is that so incredible? In my opinion she's a very fine looking woman and she wasn't always old."

"No, of course not. But—well, why have I never heard of it before?"

"Because it's not a matter we care to discuss."

"Who was the man? Was it anyone I knew?"

"I imagine you remember him quite well. It was Willie Foster-Smith."

"Foster-Smith!" A memory came to Colin of a spectacled face, of gentle, bewildered eyes, a hesitant smile, an excitable stammer. "Yes, of course I remember him. He used to come sailing with us. He rented the Robertsons' cottage here for a time, didn't he?"

"Yes, it was after the war," Clara said. "Dolly was thirty-eight. Not young exactly, but certainly not as old as

you no doubt thought her at the time. Willie was a little
younger than she was, about thirty-five, I think. Not so
much, anyway, that we thought of it as an impediment.
He'd been demobilised and didn't want to go into the
family business and he had his gratuity, so he rented the
Robertsons' cottage and tried to become a painter."

Colin nodded. " Yes, boats and storms, seagulls flying
about, lots of very purple heather. I used to think they were
terrific. What happened to him? "

" I'm afraid he didn't succeed. But that's beside the
point. It wasn't his painting we had against him. As a
matter of fact, I quite admired it. I like a picture to look like
something I can recognise. And during the two years he
lived here he and Dolly naturally saw a great deal of one
another."

" I remember that, but I never thought . . ." He gave
a laugh. " I suppose one isn't very perceptive at fourteen.
What went wrong? Why didn't they marry? "

" Because of that woman—Ginny's mother. I don't like
to speak her name. It was only a few weeks after Willie
and Dolly came to an understanding, which happened just
after you'd gone back to school, I remember. That's why
you heard nothing of it at the time. And they both decided
against any public announcement until Willie should have
come to a decision about his future—most fortunately, as it
turned out. It saved Dolly a great deal of humiliation.
But not of pain and disillusionment, of course. She discovered the affair herself. She went to the cottage one day
and found them there together . . ." A deep flush of
embarrassment and anger coloured Clara's lined face. " I
need not elaborate," she said.

" Poor Aunt Dolly—was this what was behind the
mysterious illness she had one summer? " Colin asked.

" It was. It was all but a nervous breakdown. And she
changed very much at that time. She got her cheerful

spirits back and her interest in things and she even resumed a friendship of a sort with Willie—as you know, she's always been generous to a fault—but she'd always been very independent of Phyllis and me before her illness, going off into the A.T.S. and so forth, but afterwards she began to cling to us. Of course, it may have been for the best. Willie had a weak character and he was an artist. I dare say Harriet Jerrold was neither the first nor the last. But that thought has made it no easier for me to forgive her. In my opinion she had no interest in Willie until Dolly told her of their engagement, then it was more than the creature could bear that Willie, if he was in a marrying mood, had not chosen her."

"And Foster-Smith—what happened to him?"

"Oh, he went into the family business. They manufacture woollens."

"Did he quite give up painting?"

"So far as I know, though he kept up his interest in art. He's written one or two books with names like *Artistic Treasures of Scotland,* of which he sent us autographed copies. I may say, I do not read them. I even prefer not to have them on view. . . . What's the matter, Colin? Why are you staring at me like that?"

He had not known that he was staring at her. He had been no more aware of her just then than of the fading glow in the sky or the sound of the surf, gnawing at the foot of the cliffs below them.

"Tell me," he said, "wasn't it Foster-Smith who persuaded you to have the Decayed Gentlewoman cleaned?"

"Why, yes, of course it was," said Clara.

CHAPTER ELEVEN

"And now," she said, "that I've told you what you wanted to know, are you ready to answer some questions for me?"

"Just a minute." Colin stood still, absently frowning at her. "I've got to think something out."

She propped herself against a boulder at the side of the path.

"If you think it will be too difficult for you to answer my questions, I won't ask them," she said. "I have no wish to spoil the pleasure of your visit by pressing you to tell me what you feel you would sooner not."

Colin sat down on the rock beside her. He put an arm round her.

"How would it be if I promise to tell you the whole story sometime, but only some of it now? Only as much as I'm sure of."

"Very well," she said.

He really meant as much as she needed to know. He would sooner not have told her any of it, but the Decayed Gentlewoman was back at Ardachoil, and now, for all he knew, violent men might come after her again. He had to tell his aunt of the value of the picture and the risks attached to possessing it.

But when he went on, it was to ask another question. "When Foster-Smith persuaded you to have the picture cleaned, did he give you any reason for it?"

"None in particular," she said, "except that it would be greatly improved. I had my doubts. I liked it as it was. But Phyllis and Dolly persuaded me that I was too conservative and that a man who wrote books on art must know much better than I did. No doubt they were right."

" Did he ever drop any hint who he thought the painter was? "

She shook her head. " He did say he believed the woman in the painting might be a certain Arabella Hamilton, who spent some years of her life at the court of Charles I. A very unfortunate life, he said. Her husband was killed in the Civil War and the family estates were forfeited and she and her children had to flee abroad until the Commonwealth was over. It seems Willie had looked very carefully into the whole story. I cannot say I was particularly interested. However, as you know, our grandmother was a Hamilton and I won't say there can't have been any truth in it."

" He didn't say there was a chance that the picture was extremely valuable? "

" Oh, no."

" Well now, listen," Colin said, " there is a chance that it is. There's a chance that when I was held up and my car was stolen, it was really the picture they were after, not the car."

She gave an exclamation of dismay. " But that's terrible! Are you telling me that Willie . . .? No, no, you can't mean that! You'll have gathered I've no high opinion of him, but I can't see him as a man who would steal, who would connive at your being assaulted and left untended by the roadside. Why, that might easily have been murder! "

" That's one of the things I don't want to talk about yet," Colin said, " because I don't know the truth of it myself. It's possible he only handed on the information to someone else."

" To that woman? " she asked quickly.

He stirred uneasily. " I suppose that's possible."

" In that case," she said with a certain sternness, " where does Ginny come into the affair? "

"Oh, entirely by chance," Colin answered promptly. "She happened to see the picture, recognised it——"

"Now wait a minute!" Clara said crisply. "Do you take me for a fool? If the mother was involved in the theft, it can hardly have been by chance that the daughter became involved too."

"But it was," he insisted. "Or put it like this—Ginny was the mistake they made. The slip between the cup and the lip. It never- occurred to them there was any danger in letting her see the picture. They didn't dream she'd recognise it after all these years. But she did and she immediately got in touch with me and—well, here we are."

She pursed her lips and did not reply.

He went on persuasively, "If she'd been involved, Aunt Clara, why should she have brought it back to you?"

"That's a point, certainly," she said. "It may be you're right. But you're in love with her, are you not?"

"Yes, Aunt Clara."

"It's possible that's affected your judgment."

He smiled a little. "That's a way of putting it."

"Oh, I'm serious," she said gravely. "But I admit the girl's made a far pleasanter impression on me than her mother ever did. You may be quite right about her. The question is, however, what are we to do about the picture?"

"There are two things I want to do about it," Colin said. "I want to talk to Foster-Smith and I want to talk over with a lawyer certain—well, points about the theft. And I'd be very grateful if meanwhile you'd do nothing at all except take it down again and hide it in a safe place."

"I see," she said. "Yes, I dare say that might be best. But I shall have to talk it over first with Phyllis and Dolly, to see if they agree. And there's a point you should perhaps consider, Colin. Sooner or later the police will have to hear about it all, unless the picture's to remain in concealment for ever. You know this place and how well we all know each other's business. The moment it's seen hanging where it used to be by any of our neighbours, word will go straight to Sergeant Campbell, who naturally was informed of the theft at the time. And just what action he might be compelled to take, I'm afraid I cannot tell you."

" I know—that's precisely why I want that talk with a lawyer," Colin said. " You see, there's something I haven't explained yet. Ginny and I removed the picture without asking anyone's permission. So it's just possible, if you keep it, that you'll find you're guilty of resetting stolen property."

Her blue eyes opened wide. " *We* are? Resetting . . ? But it's *our* picture! "

" Yes—there's a bit of a problem about that, however. Let me explain."

He proceeded to tell her how Edmund Greer, by purchasing the picture in a sale held regularly in a place set aside for the purpose, the sale having begun and ended in the market and taken place between sunrise and sunset, had become its legal owner.

Clara listened with deep attention. She did not interrupt, but as Colin went on, the normally ruddy tone of her complexion deepened to angry crimson.

" A fine state of affairs! " she cried. " I'm sure there's no such law as that in Scotland."

" I don't believe there is," Colin agreed. " All the same, in England the picture still belongs to Greer, unless we can prove his connection with the theft. And it was in England that Ginny and I—reappropriated it."

" You're burglars, then? "

" Well, I don't know how Scots law regards a situation like this."

" And my sisters and I . . . Resetting! Yes, certainly you must see a lawyer! "

As if she could not arrange quickly enough for him to see one, she set off quickly for home.

It was dusk when they reached the house. The copper band along the horizon had darkened to bronze and the sea grown black. Dolly was flitting round from room to room, drawing the curtains. Phyllis was in the kitchen, cooking something for supper. Ginny was curled up in a chair by the fire in the little drawing-room, asleep.

When Clara and Colin came in she started up, looked wildly round her, as if she could not think where she was, then laughed and sank back into the chair.

" I'm sorry—I thought all this was part of a dream," she said.

Clara sat down stiffly on the opposite side of the fire.

"Colin's told me how you found the picture, Ginny," she said. Her voice was far less warm than it had been before and Ginny, Colin saw, noticed it at once. Turning her head away, she looked down into the fire.

" I understand there's a possibility that it's of considerable value," Clara went on, " also that there are certain legal complications about its present ownership. In the circumstances, he's advised us to keep it concealed for the time being. I'm quite ready to fall in with his wishes, but I shall have to explain to my sisters why it seems best to do this. I don't think it's necessary to tell them the whole story, however. I don't intend to remind them that it was on the advice of Willie Foster-Smith that we sent the picture to Edinburgh to be cleaned, or that he was a friend of your mother's."

Ginny did not reply or look up.

Sounding a little flustered, as if she were beginning to wish that she had not spoken so coldly, Clara added, "That's what you'd wish yourself, isn't it, my dear? What we all want is to keep the whole affair as quiet as possible."

"Do what you think best," Ginny murmured expressionlessly.

A moment later she glanced up at Colin. He found his heart thudding. There was such black anger in her eyes that he hardly knew the face that she had raised to him.

There was nothing that he could say then. Clara was at the door, calling for Phyllis and Dolly. He made a slight gesture of helplessness. Ginny's lips formed some word that he did not hear, then she looked down at the fire again. She went on staring into it all the time that Clara was telling her sisters a carefully edited version of the story that Colin had told her.

It began with Ginny's discovery of the picture in the saleroom. That it was more valuable than any of them realised, Clara deduced simply from the fact that the bidding had gone up unexpectedly high. Then she did her best, with some help from Colin, to explain the curious situation arising from the fact that a Mr. Greer had bought the picture in the open market, and how the discovery that they could not get it back by more conventional means had led Colin and Ginny to remove it without asking anyone's permission.

"And so for their sakes it seems advisable that we should let no one know of the return of the picture until we've had time to investigate the legal position," Clara added.

By saying nothing about the original theft of the picture, she had avoided having to say anything about Willie Foster-Smith or Harriet, and Colin was just admiring the dexterity with which she had achieved this when, to his dismay, Dolly spoke up eagerly.

"Do you know what I think, Clara? I think those men who held Colin up——"

Before she could get any further, Phyllis came bursting in, "—were after the picture all the time——"

"—not the car at all!" cried Dolly. "And you see, that means——"

"—that they knew we had it!" Phyllis exclaimed.

"And do you know how I think they knew that?" Dolly demanded. Her eyes were sparkling with excitement.

"Yes, do you know?" Phyllis echoed her.

"The bee man!" they both cried together.

There was a silence. Clara put a hand to her head. For once, for just a moment, she had failed to follow her sisters' thread of thought. Then her face cleared. As eagerly as the others, she exclaimed, "Yes, yes, of course, the bee man!"

They all turned to look at Colin.

Dolly began, "It was something we never really understood."

"Though we often discussed it," said Phyllis.

"At length," said Clara.

"It was that summer, you know, before that thing happened to you," said Dolly. "We'd gone out together——"

"—to Oban," said Phyllis, "to do some shopping, only halfway there the car started giving trouble——"

"—so we turned back," said Clara.

"And as soon as we turned in at the gate," Dolly said, "the door burst open and out came——"

"—a man!" they cried in unison.

Dolly went on, "He was a bee man, with a black veil over his head, and he waved to us and called out something and went running away down the road."

"He was after his swarm, you see," said Phyllis.

"Or so we thought," said Clara.

"And of course, we followed," said Dolly.

"As fast as we could," said Phyllis. "What fun it was!"

"But he was too fast for us," Clara said with a sigh. "We never saw him again."

"And then we realised," Dolly added, "that a real bee man wouldn't have been able to unlock the door to get in. So then we thought he must have been a burglar."

"Only there was nothing missing in the house," said Phyllis.

"So then we dismissed him from our minds," said Clara.

"But now I'm sure—quite, quite *sure*," cried Dolly, "that whatever brought him, he saw that picture and made up his mind he had to have it."

There was a slight pause, then Phyllis observed thoughtfully, "An odd-looking man, was he not? I remember he seemed to lean backwards as he ran. You'd hardly think that a good way to run, but he was as swift as the wind."

"Swifter than these three old ladies, anyway," Clara said.

The sisters fell silent again and all looked expectantly at Colin.

Rather cautiously, he said, "That's very interesting. You may be right about him, Aunt Dolly. Did you ever find out how he got into the house?"

"With a skeleton key, we supposed," Dolly said. "Nothing was broken. And as long as we thought the man was only after his swarm, we didn't at all mind his having come in."

"Indeed, we were grateful," said Phyllis. "Suppose we'd come home to a kitchen swarming with bees."

"Well, I think I'd lock up and bolt the doors for the time being," Colin said. "And I think you'd better let me take the picture down again and hide it somewhere."

They agreed to do this, except that they insisted it should stay where it was for the evening.

This it did, but as soon as the sisters had gone to bed, Colin took it down, made a parcel of it with some sacking and string and carried it up to the loft. If its hiding-place behind the water tank was unlikely to save it from Edmund Greer, if he ever came looking for it again, at least there was not much chance that Sergeant Campbell would hear of it as long as it was up there.

Next morning, promising to visit his aunts' solicitors in Edinburgh as soon as they could see him and to let the aunts know the results of the interview, Colin and Ginny set off again in Harriet's car along the narrow, rough road round the loch.

Its waters were dull and grey, reflecting thick clouds moving in from the west. The air was raw and cold with a taste of rain in it. Without any sunshine, the hills had lost the wonderful colours and clear outlines of yesterday and become grey, sullen-looking masses of rock with their summits lost in mist.

Almost as sullen, Colin soon noticed, was Ginny's face. For a long time she was quite silent. Once or twice, when Colin tried to talk to her, she gave no sign that she had even heard.

" All right ! " he exploded at last, suddenly becoming intensely angry himself. " Let's talk about Foster-Smith. And your mother. And let's not forget John Clitheroe. Let's have it all out in the open. I'll tell you what I think. I think Foster-Smith discovered the value of the picture. I think he told your mother about it. I think she told Greer. I think he came up to take a look at the picture, dressed in a bee veil, agreed with Foster-Smith about what it was, held me up and did everything else, including rigging the market overt business with the Lakes. And at the time of the sale he sent your mother off to Spain to protect her, in case it could ever be said that she ought to have recognised the picture."

He paused. There was no answer.

There is nothing satisfying in conducting a quarrel with

someone who will not answer, particularly if half your attention has to be given to driving a car along a difficult road. Colin began to think he might as well lapse into a sulk himself, but there was still one thing on his mind that insisted on being said.

"Ginny, I didn't *want* to talk to Aunt Clara about your mother. But I had to tell her a good deal of the story—can't you see that? For the aunts' safety, now that they've got the picture back, they had to know the sort of man Greer is. And once I'd told Aunt Clara a little, she very quickly filled in the rest herself."

Still Ginny said nothing, but he heard her give a sigh, which was at least a response of a sort.

A few minutes later she broke her silence, to speak in a soft, detached voice, as if she were discussing the weather with a stranger.

"Colin, I know very little about the sort of work you do," she said, "but doesn't it ever happen to you that you collect a whole lot of data about something or other and then when you try to find a theory to explain things, you find there are several that seem to fit equally well?"

"Yes, of course," he said.

"And what do you do then? Do you just pick one at random, because you like it, or do you try to find out a few more facts?"

"All right, I see what you mean," he answered. "Well, when we get to Edinburgh I'm going looking for a few more facts. I'm going to call on Willie Foster-Smith. I got his address from Aunt Clara. Meanwhile, suppose you tell me the true facts about John Clitheroe."

"You're quite right about him, he doesn't exist," she said in the same remote tone.

"And—leaving out everything to do with the picture for the moment—it was through Foster-Smith you knew so much about me?"

" Yes."

" You probably know him yourself."

" Of course."

" Then in God's name," he said desperately, " why didn't you tell me so straight away?"

" Because he's quite friendly with your aunts and I didn't think that would last if they knew he still saw my mother."

" But what has that got to do with me? I thought I was supposed to be trying to help you."

" Yes, but I can't see any reason why you should know everything about me," she said, still as emotionless and mild.

" *Can't* you? " Colin was astonished at the violence that burst into his voice. " Let me tell you . . ."

But then he decided not to tell her. Not like this and not just now.

Ginny waited a moment, gave a slight shrug of her shoulders, as if she found his attitude most unreasonable, turned her head away and looked out of the side-window of the car.

After that Colin aped her withdrawal and when they talked it was like polite strangers.

They reached Edinburgh in the early afternoon. The rain had been steady for the last hour and the city was wearing its bleakest face. Princes Street was a cold grey channel of wind. The human faces in the streets looked pinched and blue. It would have seemed that the spring had been forgotten and winter come back again but for the crocuses in the grass in Charlotte Square, which Colin had to circle three times before he found a parking space near to the offices of Massie, Davitt and Gunn, W.S.

As Vickerman and Ogg to Ginny's mother, so Massie, Davitt and Gunn to Colin's aunts were names that stood for all the worldly good sense that they feared they lacked themselves. The names had been familiar to Colin all his life, but he had never yet had to pass through the dignified Adam doorway or make his way through the warren of offices concealed by the handsome stone front of the house.

Admitted by a man almost as old as the one who had admitted them at Vickerman's, he and Ginny were taken to a waiting-room as small, as dim and dusty as the other, and left there while the old man went to find out if any of the partners could see them. It all felt very much like the visit to Vickerman and Ogg, except for the splendour of the staircase up which they were presently taken, when eventually they were fetched to see Mr. Davitt.

He rose to greet them from behind a very neat desk. He was a slender, neat-looking man, who moved and spoke quietly and precisely and was very much more like what Colin felt a solicitor should be than either Mr. Ogg or Mr. Dickman, except for one thing. He had a black eye. A conspicuous, rather rakish-looking black eye. Shaking hands with Ginny and Colin and settling them in chairs on either side of the desk, he asked a few questions concerning the health of the Lockie ladies, observed that they were wonderful people, fixed Colin with his single usable eye and said, " Well now? "

Wishing that Mr. Davitt would explain the black eye, because it was a little distracting, Colin began, " I want to ask you a hypothetical question."

Mr. Davitt nodded as if he was not unaccustomed to such beginnings.

" Suppose," Colin went on, " something of some value was stolen in Scotland. Suppose it was taken to England and lost sight of there for some time——"

" One moment," Mr. Davitt interrupted. " We are not by any chance discussing the Stone, are we? "

"No," said Colin.

He thought the lawyer relaxed slightly. "Please continue."

"Suppose this thing reappeared in England," Colin said, "and was bought by somebody in the open market."

"Ah," Mr. Davitt said. "Yes. The open market."

"Suppose, in fact, it was bought in market overt."

Mr. Davitt nodded his head silently.

"That would make the purchaser the owner of this thing we're talking about, wouldn't it?"

"So I believe." The lawyer's tone conveyed that such strange foreign customs were not his province.

"Well now, suppose someone who thought that the thing still belonged to its original owners—or anyway, that it ought to, as it would if all this had happened in Scotland—suppose he took possession of it, brought it back to Scotland and returned it to them."

"I see, yes."

"What attitude do you think the Scottish police would be likely to take when the situation was brought to their attention?"

Briefly Mr. Davitt's single eye gleamed, perhaps with interest, perhaps even with amusement. Then his face regained its impersonal gravity.

"I think I should like to have notice of this question," he said. "Even then I doubt very much if I could give you anything but a very tentative answer."

"A tentative answer will do to be going on with," Colin said.

"Well, let me be sure I understand your question. When the person you referred to, who was acting on behalf of the original owners of the object in question, took possession of it after the sale, was this against the will of the purchaser in market overt?"

" Very much so."

" Well, as it happened in England, the English law would of course apply. The Scottish courts and the Scottish police would have little to do in the matter, except that the English magistrate's warrant would have to be backed by the Sheriff in whose jurisdiction the original owner was. However, I think the Sheriff would have no option but to do this. But the High Court of Justiciary has an over-riding equitable jurisdiction and it's possible that the owner might make an application to the court to prevent his being handed over."

" And what would happen then? "

" The application might or might not be successful. Such an event has never, so far as I know, happened. My own personal opinion is that it would fail, though no doubt there would be some grumbling from one or more of the judges—ineffective, of course. If the owner were handed over to the English authorities and prosecuted in an English court, I think he would be bound to be convicted."

Colin turned towards Ginny. " So there we are. It doesn't sound too good, does it? "

" Unless Greer's afraid of taking any action against us," she said. " That's what I've been counting on all along."

" Greer? " Mr. Davitt said.

" The man who bought this thing we're talking about—it's a picture—in market overt," Ginny explained. " We think he was mixed up in the theft of it from the Lockies."

" Greer," Mr. Davitt repeated thoughtfully, as if he were wondering where he had heard that name before.

" Edmund Greer," Colin said, " of Hopewood House, Hopewood, in Kent."

" Good God—Greer! " Except for the livid patch round one eye, the rest of Mr. Davitt's face turned exceed-ingly pale. " Excuse me a moment," he said, got up hurriedly and went out.

Colin and Ginny looked at one another.

"What now, I wonder," Colin said apprehensively.

In a moment Mr. Davitt returned. He was holding a copy of *The Scotsman*, fluttering the pages, hunting through them, muttering, "I'm sure . . . I'm almost sure . . . It happened to catch my eye this morning. Yes, here it is."

He folded back the pages and handed the paper to Colin, pointing at a small paragraph near the foot of one column.

Ginny got up and went behind Colin's chair to read the paragraph over his shoulder.

Under the not very arresting headline, "Murder in Kent," they read, "A body, identified as that of Mr. Edmund Greer, of Hopewood House, Hopewood, Kent, was discovered early yesterday morning at the foot of some steps leading up to the front door of his house. Death had been caused by several shots, fired at close range through the head and chest. The police wish to interview Mr. Herbert Stringer, a manservant at Hopewood House, who was last seen in the village on Monday and who it is thought may be able to help them with their inquiries. They also wish to interview a man who took a taxi from Oldersfield to Hopewood House on Monday evening, arriving there at about 8.00 p.m. He is described as six foot three inches tall, age 27-30, brown haired, wearing a grey tweed overcoat, carrying a briefcase and speaking with a Scots accent."

CHAPTER TWELVE

Colin felt Ginny's hand clutch his shoulder. She was shaking. He stood up quickly and thrust her into his chair. Her face was papery white.

"That open door . . ." she whispered. "The steps!"

Mr. Davitt reached for the newspaper, refolded it neatly and laid it down on his desk.

"You were there, then," he said.

Colin nodded without speaking.

Ginny caught hold of his hand. "He must have been there all the time, only it was so dark I didn't see him. I must have gone right past him."

"I think perhaps a cup of tea . . ." said Mr. Davitt. "Excuse me again for a moment."

As he went out, Ginny drew Colin closer to her.

"Colin, what are we going to do?"

In the midst of wondering what on earth they could do, Colin could only think about the way that she had turned to him and now rested her head against him.

"I'll have to go to the police," he said, running a finger gently through her soft hair.

"And tell them everything?"

"I suppose so. I don't know. Perhaps not. We'll have to think."

Mr. Davitt returned.

"They're sending us in some tea," he said briskly, sat down at his desk, straightened a block of paper and a couple of pencils in front of him and fixed his single clear eye on Colin. "Now don't you think it might be wise to forget hypothetical questions and tell me what really happened?"

Colin was going to agree when he felt the tightening

of Ginny's fingers on his. He changed what he had been going to say.

"I think Miss Winter and I will have to talk things over first," he said. "This news is quite a shock."

"I'm sure it is."

"I'll go to the police, of course." More than ever, Colin found himself distracted by a wish that he knew how the lawyer had come by his black eye. He couldn't see him getting it in a brawl. He couldn't see him either as the sort of man who, in absent-mindedness or intoxication, would walk into a lamp post. Yet after his own experiences of the last few days, why should either of these things seem unlikely? Nothing was quite what it seemed, apparently. Anyway, the black eye gave Mr. Davitt a rather sinister appearance as he sat watching them across his desk.

The tea was brought in. Drinking it, Ginny began to recover.

"At least it looks as if we needn't worry any more about the picture," she said.

"How do you arrive at that?" Mr. Davitt asked in a tone that sent a quiver along Colin's nerves.

"The Lockies having it back and Greer being dead," she said. "He was the only person who'd be likely to fight over market overt. Besides, whoever killed him didn't take the picture, but just left it hanging where it was, so it can't have had anything to do with his murder, can it?"

"I hope you're right." Mr. Davitt's voice was full of a profound lack of conviction. "At least let me advise you not to delay going to the police."

"Oh no, we won't." She spoke with a readiness and brightness that made Colin uneasy. She stood up. "Thank you for the tea and for telling us the worst, Mr. Davitt. I generally like knowing the worst. It's the best cure for unreasonable anxiety."

"If it *is* the worst," he said discouragingly.

He went out with them and down the handsome staircase.

At the door below, with a bitter wind, funnelled along George Street, nipping their ears, his hand at last went to his black eye. After all he was not going to let them depart with heaven knew what suspicions about how he had come by it. He touched it gingerly.

"An extraordinary thing," he observed. "I was fishing last week-end, got a fish-hook through my eyelid. Very unpleasant. But no doubt I'm lucky it was no worse. Well, let me know if I can give you any further help, Mr. Lockie, and please give my regards to your aunts."

The door closed.

Taking Ginny by the elbow, Colin hurried through the rain to the car. The world felt a little more normal than it had a moment ago and he himself a little less at sea. For a fish-hook through the eye-lid was about the one way of acquiring a black eye that did not go contrary to all his instinctive feelings about Mr. Davitt, not to mention Massie and Gunn in the background.

They got into the car. But when Colin's hand went to the ignition, Ginny caught hold of it again.

"Wait a minute," she said, "please."

Realising that he did not know where he had been thinking of going, Colin sat back and waited.

After a moment she said, "When you saw my mother— the time when you said her face had been hurt—she told you she was crying because a friend had died, didn't she?"

"Yes," he said.

She gave a shiver. "Greer!"

"I suppose it must have been," he answered unhappily.

"But she said I knew him."

"Yes, she did."

"I didn't, Colin. I never met him in my life until that beastly sale."

"Perhaps she didn't mean him, then. You said yourself

she could have had something out of the past on her mind."

"I know. But I hadn't heard about him then."

"You aren't afraid that it was she who went out there . . .?"

"No, no, no! That man must have done it, Herbert Stringer. But she must have heard about it already and she must have cared . . ." She shivered again. "I must have walked right past him in the dark. All the time I was ringing the bell and calling out to him, he must have been lying within a few feet of me."

"We'll have to go to the police," Colin said.

"Here or in Oldersfield?" she asked.

That was something that he had not thought out yet.

"I'm not sure," he said. "There's a thing I'd like to do first in any case. It won't take long and it may help us to see things more clearly."

"What is it?"

"Go to see Willie Foster-Smith."

"No," she said swiftly. "No, I won't do that. I don't want to see him."

"Why not?"

"Because I don't."

"Ginny——"

"Oh, please try to understand," she implored. "I couldn't go to see anybody at the moment. I'm feeling horribly scared and rather ill. I'd like to go somewhere quiet and try to calm down and think rationally about what I ought to do. Not necessarily what you ought to do. The two things may be quite different."

He frowned helplessly at the rain-streaked windscreen.

"Well, would you wait for me while I go to see Foster-Smith?" he asked.

"Here?" She looked round inside the little car with desperation on her face.

"You could go to my rooms," he said. "Will you go there and wait for me?"

She hesitated, then nodded. "How do I get there?"

"The easiest thing will be to take a taxi." He started the car. "There's a rank over there. I'll take you to it and I'll follow you as soon as I can. I'll probably not be long."

"You don't know Willie," she said. "If he talks at all, you won't be able to stop him."

That was more or less how Colin remembered him too. Foster-Smith had been diffident but excitably emotional, silent or stammeringly confused if there was more than one other person in the room, but eager to pour out his heart to any single listener. Perhaps a rather tiresome man, really, though pleasant with children, and almost certainly wax in the hands of a woman like Harriet Winter.

Unless it had been the other way round.

Colin realised that he found it difficult to imagine Harriet as anything but wax herself. Soft, melting wax, yielding warmly and easily to any will stronger than her own.

He gave his key to Ginny, saw her into a taxi, gave the driver his address, got back into the Mini-Minor and started out for the address that Clara Lockie had given him.

Foster-Smith lived in a stone-built Victorian terrace in Morningside. All the windows of his house were heavily veiled in net, which gave it a primly secretive look, to which the untrodden white of the doorstep and the brilliance of the brass knocker added little touches of cautious pride. Colin tried the knocker when ringing the bell three times had brought no response. He felt as if the clatter that he made must rouse the street, yet when the sound died, he heard no sound of movement in the house.

He was turning away, wondering how soon it would be worth coming back to try again, when he saw the door had silently opened a few inches and that a woman was looking out at him.

She was grey-haired and dressed in black. Her face was white, except for the redness of recent tears round her eyes. She gave Colin a dazed, questioning look and said huskily, " Yes? "

" Is is possible for me to see Mr. Foster-Smith? " he asked.

" Mr. Foster-Smith? " she echoed vacantly.

" Yes. My name's Lockie—Colin Lockie. I'm not sure if he'll remember me. It's a long time since we met. But he knows my family. If I could see him for a few minutes . . ."

" No," she said. " No, no, no."

She started to close the door.

Colin did not quite put his foot in it, but he went so close to the opening that instinctively she took a step back.

" It won't take long," he said. " I think he'd probably want to see me."

She shook her head. Her swollen eyes filled with tears.

" Then you haven't heard . . . I suppose it's my fault." She spoke in an almost inaudible whisper. " I'm his sister, you see. His only sister."

Colin's heart missed a beat. " Has something happened to him, Miss Foster-Smith? "

" Yes, on Monday. They told me he was improving, so I came home. I'd been there at the hospital almost all the time since the accident. I hadn't had any sleep for— oh, I don't know how long it was. I've got in a muddle about everything." Her hand went to her forehead. " But they said he was improving, so I came home. I wouldn't have, if I'd known. I'd have stayed."

" He died? " Colin asked. " On Monday? "

She nodded.

" After an accident? "

"Yes. He went out to take the dog for a little walk before going to bed—he always does—did. Lockie, you said?" His name seemed at last to reach her consciousness. "That's the name of those friends of his in the West, isn't it?"

"Yes."

"Come in, Mr. Lockie. I'd have asked you in at once, only I'm so confused." She opened the door wider, moving to one side so that Colin could come in, then she closed it again as softly and as quietly as she had opened it and tiptoed across a narrow hall to a door. "The funeral's tomorrow," she said. "People say you feel better after the funeral, when it's all finished and done with. I don't know."

Feeling brutal at forcing himself on her, but that now it was more important than ever to find out certain things, Colin followed her into a big, unheated room and took the chair she indicated beside the empty fireplace. There was a chill in his veins already because of what she had told him, which the cold of the room seemed to magnify almost to a pain. He supposed it was the ache of a kind of fear, of horror at having to face the facts that he had already guessed. He looked round the room so that he could avoid looking too steadily at the woman's grief-stricken face.

It was a collector's room, so full of furniture, of china, of glass, of pictures, of cases full of ancient coins, of embroidered samplers, that to do any living in it, even any quiet talking with friends, would probably create fearful hazards for its contents. But Colin could easily visualise the man whom he remembered moving around eagerly and delicately, duster in hand, and when everything had been picked up, caressed with the duster and put down again, going back to the beginning and starting all over again.

"Yes," Miss Foster-Smith said in her husky whisper, following Colin's glance about the room. "He had some beautiful things. They were his great interest in life. He used to paint himself and very nicely too, but he was so critical, he was never satisfied, so he almost gave it up. But he went on writing about art. You know his books, I expect."

Colin nodded, seeing no need to tell her that he had heard of them for the first time the day before.

"Miss Foster-Smith, could you tell me a little more about your brother's accident?" he said. "My aunts were very attached to him. I'd like to be able to tell them what happened."

"He was very fond of them too," she murmured. "I thought at one time . . . But that's a long time ago. They stayed good friends. He had a lot of woman friends. They liked him. He was always so loyal and so considerate."

"When did the accident happen?" Catching himself whispering, like her, Colin realised that even without death in the air, it would have seemed natural to whisper in that room, in case a word, ringing out too loudly, should shatter something precious.

"It was Tuesday," she answered. "A week ago yesterday. I don't know what happened. Nobody saw it. They just found him, some neighbours, by the letter-box at the end of the road. The dog, poor little Tinker, was killed outright. The police blamed it all on Tinker. They said he must have run out into the road and Willie made a grab to save him and the car swerved and lost control . . . But they might have stopped, mightn't they? Wasn't it a wicked thing to drive straight on?"

"It was."

Colin was thinking of Harriet, sitting alone in the dark with her scratched face, weeping for a friend who had died. Not Greer, but Willie Foster-Smith. Had she tried to telephone to him on Monday and been told the news of his death? Had she rushed round to the Lakes then to accuse them of murder and been hurt and threatened for her pains?

Miss Foster-Smith was saying, "I don't really believe it was like that at all, of course. But it's no use arguing, is it? Besides, all this week I haven't done much but pray. While there was life there was hope, they told me. So I prayed. It was all I could do. His skull was fractured and there were other injuries. They operated. They said there was hope. Then they said he was better. So I came home and went to sleep. And when I woke up he was dead. If I'd known he was going to die, I wouldn't have left him."

Colin sensed in a way it felt less grievous to her to explore her own shortcomings than to fix her mind on the sheer emptiness of loss.

He asked, "What do you mean when you say you don't believe it happened like that?"

"Tinker was such a good little dog," she said. "He was very well trained. Very obedient. When Willie took him out he used to stick at his heels and didn't go off the pavement unless Willie said he could."

"So you don't think he dashed in front of a car."

"I do not. I think some drunken wretch was driving who went up on to the pavement and mowed them both down—Willie and Tinker—as they were quietly walking along. And then he drove on and never looked back. God knows, perhaps he didn't even know what he'd done. Perhaps in the morning he didn't even remember it."

"I think he did," Colin muttered. "Did you tell the police your idea?"

"I told the Procurator Fiscal when he came to see me.

He said I might be right. He said in any case they'd go on looking for the driver and the car. But I know he thought it was Tinker. What do you think, Mr. Lockie? "

" I don't think it was Tinker."

By contrast with the desolation in her face, the slight change in its expression seemed almost like a smile. " I'm very glad to hear you say that. He was such a good little dog and devoted to Willie, as Willie was to him."

Colin stood up. He thanked her for having talked to him and said good-bye. As before, when she had let him in, she tiptoed softly ahead of him to the door and opened and closed it softly as if she feared to waken a sleeper in the house.

Once outside, the feeling of cold at his heart melted in the throbbing of anger. He felt sick with it as he strode to the gate. He fumbled with the latch and could not get it open. Then he could not find the car-keys in his pocket. Standing beside the car, he cursed in tense, shaking rage.

Greer was dead now, but there was still Herbert Stringer. There were still the Lakes. And Harriet Winter—only he no longer felt that he knew where he was with Harriet. But if she was involved in this, she need expect no mercy. Everything must be dragged into the open now. And for everything, from the attack on him two years ago to that woman's grief, those guilty should be made to pay.

The keys had slipped through a hole in a pocket and secreted themselves cunningly in the lining of his jacket. It took some deftness to extricate them. By the time he had done it and started the car, his breathing was more normal, but the set of his mouth was still strange as he drove off.

The house where he had lived for the last year was only ten minutes' drive away. He started off recklessly, then checked himself, and aware of his tension, drove more slowly than usual. When he stopped the car at the gate, he saw his landlady, Mrs. MacGarvey, sitting at her window. As soon as she saw him she made some excited signs to him, heaved her bulk out of her armchair and vanished.

Since he had given Ginny his latch-key, he had been intending to ring the bell, but now he waited for Mrs. MacGarvey, to find out what had so wrought her up. Appearing at the door, she came close to him, and although there was no one near to hear her, put her mouth to his ear.

"There's a lady upstairs, doctor," she breathed into it. "I was in two minds, should I let her in or no. But she said you'd be expecting her."

"Yes," Colin said, "that's all right, Mrs. MacGarvey."

"I said you were away. I said I didn't know when you'd be back. She said she would wait."

"Yes," he said and tried to pass her.

But her width took up most of the passage inside.

"She's a mind of her own, doctor," she said. "I'd not have let her in if she'd given me time to think. I wouldn't let anyone into your bedroom without instructions. But she was right sharp with me and up the stairs before I knew what she was doing."

"It's quite all right, Mrs. MacGarvey," he said. "I asked her to come here."

"And then this came for you." She picked up a folded note that had been lying on the hall table. "Pushed in at the letter-box. I happened not to be in my room, so I didn't see who brought it."

Colin glanced at it, saw that it was addressed to him in a writing that he did not know, thrust it into a pocket, managed at last to edge round Mrs. MacGarvey and went running up the stairs.

There were lights on the stairs and landings, but none in his room. There was only the red oblong of the gas fire. That for the moment made it possible for him to think that it was Ginny whose head and shoulders he saw, outlined in the dusk against the window. Then a movement of the shoulders, too rigid for Ginny, and a gleam of jewelled spectacles warned him.

Switching on the light, he said, " It isn't here, Mrs. Lake. But I suppose you've found that out already."

CHAPTER THIRTEEN

BERYL LAKE did not move except to take off her spectacles and spin them idly round by one of the ear-pieces. Without them her shortsightedness very slightly softened the intentness of her gaze, but her eyes still had a pebbly hardness. She was wearing a lilac tweed overcoat with a narrow mink collar and some heavy silver ear-rings.

" I didn't think it would be here," she said. " I came to talk to you."

Trying to mask the sick anxiety he felt, not because Beryl was here, but because Ginny wasn't, Colin shut the door behind him.

" Did you tell my landlady I was expecting you?" he asked.

" Weren't you? " she said.

" Sometime, I suppose. You or one of the others."

" What others? "

" Your husband or Stringer. I may as well tell you, Mrs. Lake, I believe I've sorted out most of the plot. There won't be much point in our talking if you don't face that."

" So Ginny told you? "

" Ginny? "

She did not answer, but only gave him a mock-gentle smile as she spun the flashing spectacles round and round.

" Where is she now?" he asked. " What have you done with her? "

"I haven't seen her," Beryl said. "Not for days."

"But she was coming here . . ."

Suddenly Colin remembered the note in his pocket, pulled it out and opened it up.

Beryl went on, "You'd probably find a drink as welcome as I should. Haven't you something on the premises?"

Colin was reading, "Darling Colin—I know you don't like that word, but it's derived from the Saxon deórling, which surely gives it a respectable ancestry and even then it meant dearly beloved—I looked this up in a dictionary at Ardachoil while you were out walking with Aunt Clara—you do see, don't you, that the best thing is for me to go straight back? Otherwise you'll only get pulled deeper and deeper in and you needn't pretend to me you're going to like it. It's sure to do you harm too in your sort of job, if it hasn't already. I can probably cope with everything if you'll just stay away. I mean this, Colin deórling. Apart from all this, I'd have liked to stay—you don't know how much. But I'm going to push this in at your letter-box and make for the station. The taxi-driver says there's a good train to London at four. I think I can just make it. With all my love—if it's any good to you—Virginia."

It was an almost unreadable scrawl and must have been written hurriedly in the jolting taxi. As Colin finished it, he could think only of one thing and that was that all this time Ginny had been wanting to be called Virginia. Not a useful thing to start thinking about with Beryl Lake sitting there, her sharp gaze pinned to his face.

He folded the note and put it back in his pocket.

"A drink—there may be something," he said vaguely.

Nobody that he could remember had ever called Ginny Virginia. So her use of the name now felt like the offer of something that she did not give to other people. But the wretched girl must be half-way to Newcastle by now and that wasn't going to help in the least.

Opening a cupboard, he brought out a bottle of whisky that had been there since Christmas and was still half full. He poured some into two glasses, gave one to Beryl and with the other went to stand in front of the gas fire.

"I've just been to see Miss Foster-Smith," he observed. Beryl drank avidly.

"Foster-Smith—that seems to ring a bell," she said.

"You surprise me!" He put his glass down after only just putting it to his lips. He found that he could not face the idea of drinking with Beryl.

"I've a feeling I'm going to surprise you still more shortly," she said. "I'm afraid you're a rather simple young man."

"I don't doubt it," he answered.

"What about this Miss Foster-Smith?"

"She was grieving for her murdered brother. Odd thing to do, I expect you think—but there you are, it's the sort of woman she is."

"Would you mind explaining what you're talking about?" she said.

"Yes, I do mind explaining what you already know."

She looked at him thoughtfully. "I suppose if I say I don't know, you won't believe me."

"No," he said.

"All the same, the only murder I've heard of recently was down our way. The murder of Mr. Greer, in whom you were taking such an interest a few days ago. You've heard of it, I imagine."

"Yes."

"Do you know the police are looking for a tall man with a Scots accent?"

"Yes."

"Do you mean to go to them?"

"Yes, I do."

" I don't see why you should," she said. " You had nothing to do with it."

" But I may be able to help them with their inquiries. I've begun to look forward to doing that."

She searched his face for a moment, then with an odd little smile, said, " If that's true, Mr. Lockie, I've been mistaken about you and I may as well go home again. I'd hoped we were going to be able to come to some arrangement."

" After two murders? "

" Two—? " She said it as if she thought that she had not heard him correctly.

Colin found it an effort to keep his voice from shaking. "Damn it, I don't care what you did to Greer! But to kill poor Willie Foster-Smith and his poor damned little dog! To mow them down in cold blood, almost as you did me when you first grabbed the picture, only this time meaning to kill! "

" *I* did these things?" she said in amazement. " *I'm* going around murdering people? "

" It may have been Greer or Stringer, but you knew all about it. Listen, Mrs. Lake——" Colin's anger was beginning to get out of control, which scared him when he became aware of it. He started to walk up and down the room, keeping his clenched fists in his pockets. "Whatever good you think you can do here, it won't help you not to recognise how much I know. I know Willie Foster-Smith spotted the picture at Ardachoil for what it was. I know he told Mrs. Winter about it. I know she told Greer— or perhaps she told you and your husband and you told Greer. I know Greer went to Ardachoil, broke into the house and had a look at the picture, decided Foster-Smith was right about it, found out when I was going to take it to Edinburgh, held me up and stole it. After that he kept it out of sight for a couple of years, waiting till it had had a chance to be forgotten and till you had a houseful of stuff like Mrs. Sibbald's to sell. You slipped it inconspicuously in among the junk then and put it up for auction. But before that——" Colin had come to a standstill in front of the gas fire again. "Before that Foster-Smith had to be killed. If the picture had ever come up for sale at Sotheby's, he'd have recognised it and if he'd ever found out that Greer had bought it in a saleroom next to Mrs. Winter's café, he could hardly have let it pass without starting a full scale investigation. And that would have spoiled all the carefully worked out market overt set-up."

Without disputing anything that he had said, Beryl remarked, "It's interesting that you still don't seem to know what the picture is."

"I don't," he said.

"It's a Rubens."

"A—?"

"Oh yes," she said, almost casually. "Your friend Foster-Smith had his suspicions years ago and set about tracking down the history of the painting. It's the portrait of a woman called Arabella Hamilton, whom Rubens painted when he came to the court of Charles I in 1629 for an eight months' visit. He did a number of portraits during that time—Foster-Smith, of course, knew that and he dug up a lot of information about the Hamilton family, which made him sure he was on the right track. For your information, it's probably worth around thirty thousand pounds or more."

"In the open market?"

She smiled sardonically. "Naturally. Well, Mr. Lockie?"

"What do you mean—well?"

"I was just wondering if you mightn't feel a little

tempted. To co-operate, I mean, without letting your relatives know too much about it. However, I can see it was a stupid idea."

" It strikes me as rather stupid too to call it a Rubens," Colin said. " It's not in the least like one."

" Because you expect Rubens to be all great slabs of pink flesh? You're quite wrong. Rich and wonderful, yes, and you'll find out Arabella turns out a lot richer, a lot more wonderful than you expect when she's been cleaned up. Oh yes, indeed. But if you doubt me, I can probably find the letter Foster-Smith wrote to Harriet that gave all the details of his research. Greer was satisfied, anyway, and he was quite an expert." With a quick little movement she put her spectacles on again, as if to make a specially careful study of the effect on Colin of what she was going to say next. " I'm talking about the letter, Mr. Lockie, that Ginny brought to us."

Colin said nothing. He knew that for the moment it was the only thing to do. He had to keep his teeth together and the tumult inside him to himself.

Beryl drank some more whisky, laughed and said, " And I was fully expecting to have my head bitten off! I keep being wrong about you."

" Go on! " he managed to say.

" You're sure you want me to? "

" Go on! "

" About the letter? Well, you don't suppose Harriet had the brains to see the possibilities, do you? She's far too ignorant and feeble-minded. But Ginny's shrewd, well educated, well informed. She may not have let you notice that. She tends not to. Poor little lost soul, Ginny—that's the picture of herself she likes people to have. In fact she got a good degree at Bristol, I think it was, and teaches English in some quite classy girls' school. But she'd like to do better for herself. She's told me she feels the life cramps her style. And when Ginny wants a thing, she goes after it."

Ginny's note crackled in Colin's pocket as he crushed it in his hand.

" Well? " he said.

" Haven't I told you enough? Have I got to tell you all the miserable details? "

" You seem to be trying to tell me Ginny was in on the whole thing."

" From the very beginning."

" Then why did she wreck it by getting in touch with me? "

" Because Greer blundered."

" How? "

" By trying to edge her out of the big deal. He argued she'd done none of the planning and taken none of the risks. If things went wrong, she wouldn't even be involved. So she ought to be satisfied, he said, with two or three hundred pounds at most and if she didn't like it, he'd let Stringer loose on her. I told him he was making a mistake. I told him she'd be very angry and she wouldn't intimidate easily. She wasn't a soft dollop of dough like Harriet that you could kick around without her ever trying to get back at you. But he was never very good with women. He never understood what made them tick. He didn't see that a couple of hundred was almost worse than nothing to Ginny—an insult, really."

She put down her empty glass and rested her head on her hand.

" I know I'd have felt just as she did," she went on. " All the same, I never thought she'd do what she did, I mean, bring you in. When she started bidding at the sale, I thought it was just showing her teeth, giving Greer a bit of warning that she was around. But that she'd blow the whole thing sky-high by getting hold of you just never occurred to me."

"So you blundered too," Colin said.

"That's right, I did. But not like Greer. He made the really fatal blunder."

"So fatal," Colin said, "that I wonder if he made it."

She reached for her glass again, saw it was empty, put it down and to have something to do with her nervous hands, started adjusting the screw of one of her heavy silver ear-rings.

"You probably don't believe any of this," she said. "I didn't really expect you to. Not at first."

"Greer didn't strike me as a fool." Colin was pleased with the appearance of calm that he had achieved. "And to cut Ginny out when, as you say he pointed out, she wouldn't even be involved if things went wrong, seems just too stupid for him to have done it."

"I told you, he thought she could be scared," Beryl said. "If not directly herself, then through Harriet. He *was* a fool, a stupid fool who'd never listen to anyone else! That's why he's dead!" There was suddenly rage in her voice. "As if he could ever get at Ginny through Harriet. She doesn't give a damn for her—never has. D'you think she'd even have been looking after the café for her if she hadn't known the sale was coming off that week?" She picked up her glass and pounded with it on the table. "Oh, for God's sake, give me another drink!"

Colin refilled her glass. "Why is Greer dead, Mrs. Lake? Why did you have to kill him?"

"*I?*" she said shrilly. "Haven't I said I don't go around murdering people? I can prove it too. Luckily I've a very sound alibi for the whole of that evening."

"Supplied by Mrs. Winter? Didn't she come to see you?"

"I don't have to rely on her. Joe and I were working in

the saleroom all the evening, sorting out some new stuff. So the lights were on and anyone crossing the square would have seen us." She drank some whisky. " Stringer killed him."

" Why? "

" My idea is that he got scared when he found you were coming back to Oldersfield, so he decided to get out, helping himself to what he could before he went. And Greer came in in the middle. Going by the papers—because naturally we haven't been hanging around the place ourselves and the police haven't got round to our connection with Greer yet—his safe had been opened and was empty and one or two locked cupboards had been broken open and everything inside messed about."

" Why didn't Stringer take the picture? "

" Too dangerous, perhaps. He may not have known where to sell it either. Of course . . ." She paused. " There's another possible explanation. Perhaps he didn't take the picture because it was gone already."

Colin nodded. " I thought we were coming to that."

She gave a smile which was almost sympathetic. " Oh, I wish you'd be your age, you poor thing! Haven't you realised yet your turning up at Hopewood upset Ginny's plans as badly as all of ours? "

" How? "

" Well, she wasn't expecting you, was she? I've been talking to Harriet, so I know that. You didn't come back to Oldersfield with Ginny, you came some time later. You weren't even sure where she'd gone when you took that taxi to Hopewood. You were simply going looking for her."

" Well? "

" So you must have met her somewhere when she was getting away with the picture and what could she do then but pretend she was taking it back to your aunts? "

" Having just murdered Greer? "

" I haven't said so."

" Isn't it the idea you've been working round to? "

" I tell you, I don't know." There was a touch of fretfulness in her voice. " It's true there are some things I don't understand about the whole set-up. But if Greer wasn't dead already when Ginny arrived, how did she get away with the picture—unless she killed him herself? If he was dead already, on the other hand, how did she manage not to fall over his body? It was found right at the bottom of the front steps."

" Falling over his body wouldn't have been murder," Colin said.

" True. But walking straight past it wasn't such a very nice thing to do, was it? Not just the sort of thing a judge will commend her for at the trial."

" So now we've got to the trial. What comes next? The deal you're ready to make? There has to be a reason why you're telling me so much."

She stood up swiftly, came close to him and looked up at him with a brilliant smile.

" You aren't taking me in, Mr. Lockie," she said. " You're being very calm, very unmoved. But what's behind it? All kinds of things and none of them pleasant. Of course you don't believe more than a quarter of the things I've been telling you. You're in love with the girl and the girl Mr. Lockie's in love with isn't a thief or a murderess. All right, let's say she isn't. I'm quite ready to leave you to solve your personal problems yourself. What I tell you though is that if you don't get me the picture back, the police are going to hear all about Ginny's visit to Hopewood. They're going to hear all about her showing me the letter from Foster-Smith. They're going to hear the story just as I've told it to you."

" How can you tell them that without getting into trouble yourself, Mrs. Lake? "

" It'd be nothing like the trouble Ginny would get into—a thought that would compensate for quite a lot! "

Her closeness was working on Colin's temper. He could feel the heat of hatred coming from her, inflaming the anger in himself. But in the same level tone as before, he remarked, " You've a tremendous confidence in love, Mrs. Lake. Do you really think I'd trade a picture worth thirty thousand pounds for a girl who's done the things you've told me? "

She laughed abruptly. " I told you, you aren't taking me in. You'll trade it to protect your faith that she didn't do them. To protect yourself from having it all thrashed out in court. From having to face the truth they may arrive at."

" No," he said.

" I'm not taking no for an answer."

" Then I suppose you'll have to do without one."

" That's quite all right for the moment," she said. " It's what I was expecting. I'm going to give you a little time to think it over. You can have till this evening. Then if you don't give me the answer I want, you'll be in for trouble—you and Ginny."

She went to the door.

" I'll be back about ten o'clock," she added over her shoulder.

CHAPTER FOURTEEN

COLIN DRANK his whisky. It warmed his anger, gave it a sustaining strength, made decisions easy. He went downstairs. There was a telephone in the hall for the use of Mrs. MacGarvey's lodgers. It was uncomfortably public, but he had no time to worry about that. He dialled the operator and gave her the Ardachoil number.

Clara Lockie answered the telephone.

"Aunt Clara—this is Colin," he said and cut short the question she immediately started to ask him about whether he had yet been to Massie, Davitt and Gunn. "Listen, I want you to do something and do it immediately. I want you to get the picture down out of the loft, take it along to Sergeant Campbell, tell him I brought it, that it's very valuable, that you're afraid to keep it and that he must keep it in the police-station, or send someone with you while you take it to the bank. Tell him you think there may be an attempt to steal it again. Then get out of the house yourselves. Go and stay with some friends for the next few days."

There was a slight pause, then Clara said, "And you— when will you be back?"

"Not immediately. But will you do as I say?"

"Are you sure it's necessary?"

"I am."

"I must, of course, discuss it with the others."

"All right—so long as you make them do it, Aunt Clara." He had just time to feel thankful that the aunts were too economical to have extensions to their telephone, otherwise he would have found himself having to persuade all three at once in one of their odd, shared-out conversations. "I'm very serious. There's something else I've got to tell you, then you can tell Aunt Dolly. It's about Willie Foster-Smith."

"Yes?" she said.

"He's dead. He was smashed up in a car accident last week. He died on Monday. I saw his sister this afternoon."

There was another pause. It lasted long enough for him to think that perhaps she had left the telephone.

"Aunt Clara!" he said.

"Yes, dear," she answered. "I won't ask you to tell me the rest of it now, but it was connected, was it not?"

"I think so. So you'll understand the importance of

doing what I say. One of them—the people involved—was here just now. She'd been hunting for the picture. When I walked in, she told me a yarn about it that was supposed to keep me here for the evening while she or one of the others got over to Ardachoil. That's what I make of it, anyway."

"I see. But about the legal position, Colin——"

"Don't bother about it. It doesn't matter any more. The picture's yours."

"And you and Ginny are not going to get into trouble?"

He swallowed. "Not the slightest, Aunt Clara."

"Then good-bye just now."

"Good-bye."

He put the telephone down and turned. He had heard the sound of someone breathing heavily behind him.

"Oh, Dr. Lockie, I couldn't help overhearing," Mrs. MacGarvey said. "Did I do wrong, letting that woman in? I'd never have let her get by if I'd had time to think, but she was up the stairs before I knew what she was at."

"No, it's quite all right, I'm glad I had a chance to talk to her," he answered. "I've got to go out again now. I don't suppose you could cash a cheque for me, could you, Mrs. MacGarvey?"

"A cheque?" she said, wrinkling her forehead. "How much would it be for?"

"I need about ten pounds."

"Ten pounds—oh, I've nothing like that! I could let you have three or four, maybe."

"That's better than nothing." He took his cheque book from his pocket.

But when she brought him the three pounds ten that she decided she could spare, she told him not to bother with a cheque, but to pay her back when he had it. Colin stuffed the notes into his wallet, went out to the car and drove to the garage where he usually had his own car

serviced. They cashed a cheque for five pounds. Thinking
that now he could just manage, he drove to Turnhouse
Airport.

All this time he was possessed by a feeling of complete
certainty. He was completely certain that Beryl had been
looking for the picture in his room, that her next step
would be to look for it at Ardachoil, that for the sake of
the safety of the three women there he had had to make the
telephone call to Aunt Clara, that Ginny herself would have
done the same, if she had been here. In fact, that call
had been the clearest gesture of confidence in Ginny that he
had known how to make.

It was only when he was in the aeroplane on the way
back to London, with nothing to do for the next hour but
sit still, that the first doubts came trickling into his mind.
Had he acted like a madman? Ought he to have stayed
to hear what Beryl had to say when she returned at ten
o'clock?

Only she wasn't going to return. But suppose she did . . .

All of a sudden something that he had been trying not
to think about pushed its way into his mind, filled it, allowed
room for nothing else. It was the thought of Ginny's crazy
driving as they tore away from Hopewood, of her stopping
the car and diving behind the hedge to be sick.

" What of it? " his rational mind asked.

He would probably be sick himself after committing his
first burglary. But his memory and his imagination began
to touch in the details of a picture of Greer's house, of the
doorway and the steps and of a body lying at the bottom
of the steps. It had been a dark night, but the walk from
the gate to the door was long enough for Ginny's eyes to
have adjusted themselves somewhat to the darkness and if
the door had been ajar, as she had said, some light from
the opening would have fallen across the steps, would even
have seemed bright after the blackness. And if there had

been a strange shape lying at the bottom of the steps in that shaft of light, how could she have missed seeing it? Even if Greer's body had fallen to one side of the steps, Colin thought that it would still have been visible. To try to ignore that fact would not be useful.

As the plane droned on through the darkening sky, and afterwards, when he was in the bus to Cromwell Road, then in the taxi to King's Cross, where he was waiting at the barrier when Ginny came off the train from Edinburgh, Colin kept returning to the problem of what she had really seen. But when she caught sight of him standing there, when she gave a start and flushed pink, then darted towards him and clung to him as if he were the source of all strength and all safety, the questions that he had been preparing to ask her simply faded from his mind.

" I'd been hoping you'd be here," she said with her face against him, " although I didn't see how you could be. I've been feeling such a fool for going off like that. But it seemed the only thing to do at the time. I meant to cope on my own."

" That's a rather bad habit you've got," he mumbled happily.

" Yes, isn't it? Well, what are we going to do now? Go to the police, or flee abroad together? "

" We might be able to fit in both with a little organisation. But I'm afraid the police will have to come first."

" In Oldersfield? "

" I suppose so."

" In that case, we could look in on my mother first, couldn't we? "

" Yes, I think we should," he answered. " I think if we can find out a certain thing from her, we ought to be able to tell the police quite a lot."

" I've been thinking hard for the last six hours," Ginny

went on as they walked to the taxi-queue. "A train, when you're alone, is a good place for thinking."

"So is a plane," said Colin.

"I've been thinking however irresponsible she is—I'm talking about Mother—she doesn't do deliberately evil things. In a certain sense, you can trust her. I believe so, anyway. So I've been making up my mind, even if things look bad, I'm *going* to trust her. It's a thing you have to do with everyone you know at some point—make up your mind about that, I mean."

With his eyes on her face, which looked very tired in spite of the pink flush of excitement, Colin replied, "Yes, I know."

"And that means that even if she knew Greer and was crying because she'd heard he was dead, I haven't got to be afraid she's mixed up in things so deeply that I daren't tell the truth about what I know."

"Ginny, she wasn't crying for Greer," Colin said. "She probably didn't know he was dead. She may not even have known him."

"But you told me she said she was crying for someone who'd died."

"Yes, but it was for Willie Foster-Smith. He was knocked down by a car last week and died on Monday. She must have tried to ring him up for some reason that day, while you were in London, and been told the news by his sister."

He saw the shock on Ginny's face. Her lips fumbled soundlessly with the word, "Willie?"

He went on quickly, "It was all arranged while she was abroad, Ginny—his death and the sale. I'm sure now she didn't know anything about it till she came back. She may not even understand what happened."

"Then it was murder?"

"I'm sure it was."

"Because he would have recognised the picture when Greer put it up for sale?"

He nodded.

"And we don't even know yet what the picture is."

"Beryl says it's a Rubens."

They were at the head of the queue now and a taxi was coming towards them. Ginny had been stepping off the kerb, but she spun round to face him again.

"When did you see Beryl?"

He took her by the arm, opened the door of the taxi, thrust her in and told the driver to take them to Charing Cross.

"I found her in my room after I'd been to see Miss Foster-Smith," he said.

"And she told you the picture was a Rubens?"

"And a lot of other things, which I've had time to think over on the plane. I came to almost the same conclusion as you came to on the train."

"What do you mean?" she asked.

"That there's always a point when you have to make up your mind how far you trust a person."

"Trust Beryl, do you mean?"

"I do not." He reached for her, gathering her into his arms. "Can we forget Beryl for a bit?"

"I can easily forget her for always, if you can."

"There's just one thing . . ."

"What?"

"Ginny, is it true you're a schoolmistress?"

Drawing closer to him, she gave a muffled laugh. "Yes, it is."

"Well, God damn it, why make a secret of it? What's the matter with it?"

"Nothing, except that I'm rather too proud of it," she said. "In a private sort of way. I mean that I've turned out quite good at it and that I'm capable of sticking to it. I'm slowly finding out that I'm a much more stable character than I ever used to think. But it's such a precious discovery, I think it's safer not to talk about it. And if that sounds like nonsense to you——"

" It doesn't."

" Well, whether it does or not, there's the point that I can't let the two lives overlap, can I? I expect that's obvious. I don't actually enjoy keeping them so separate, but it seems to be the only solution for the present." She was silent for a moment. " Colin, in spite of what I said just now about trusting Mother, I'm still frightened for her. I'm worried about Joe too."

" Why about Joe? "

" Because I've known him so long and I seem to have been so wrong about him."

" Perhaps you haven't been. Perhaps he's perfectly honest after his own fashion."

" But if he's mixed up in this . . ."

" I've been wondering if he really is, anyway in quite the way I thought. D'you remember the day you took me round to see them? D'you remember how Beryl stayed out of the office, as if she'd no interest in what was happening? "

" Yes, and you could see that bright green suit of hers through the hinge of the door. You asked me why she should pretend not to be interested, when we could see she was there, listening."

" The point is, I don't think Joe could see her, so it could have been done to impress Joe, not us. Then, when she came in, they disagreed about which of them had suggested buying the contents of the Sibbald house outright, instead of selling it on commission. It was important to buy it outright, of course, with the picture in with the rest. But Beryl was very sharp with Joe, trying to make him think it was his idea."

"Then do you think it's possible he still doesn't know that Beryl was in with Greer?"

"That's one of the things I want to ask your mother. She knows him pretty well, doesn't she?"

"Yes, and she's fond of him. But, Colin——"

"Yes."

"I kept thinking all the time I was on the train. I just don't believe Greer's body could have been at the bottom of the steps when I went into the house. I'd have seen it, if it had been."

Colin hesitated, then said, "Yes, I think so too."

"So why was the door open?" she asked. "I thought at first Greer must have rushed out, trying to get away from Stringer, and Stringer must have shot him as he was running down the steps, then done a bolt himself without thinking about the door. But if Greer's body wasn't there when I arrived—and I'm really sure it can't have been— and if the murder really happened after I left, where were they both when I got there? And why did Stringer leave the picture behind?"

"I've an idea," Colin said slowly, "that the murder had nothing to do with the picture. Nothing, that is, to do with the possession of the picture."

"I don't understand."

"I'm not sure that I do either. It's a very hazy idea. Let's leave it till we've seen your mother. Then perhaps we'll know a bit more."

They did not reach Oldersfield till nearly midnight. The train that they had found waiting at Charing Cross, due to leave in seven minutes, was a very slow one, stopping at every small station. Ginny dropped off to sleep with her head on Colin's shoulder. When at last he had to rouse her, she got up, yawning and confused. But when she had taken a few breaths of the cold spring night, she became restlessly alert. Walking fast through the quiet streets of the town, they set off for the Green Tree Café.

Its door was locked, and its window was dark. Only the street-lamps in the market place lit up the sponge cakes and biscuits on the glass shelves. The same sponge cakes and biscuits, it occurred to Colin, while Ginny was feeling in her handbag for her key, as had been there when he first came to the café.

But light showed dimly through the curtains of the barred basement window. Harriet was there.

Ginny opened the door and Colin followed her.

Halfway across the empty, shadowy room inside, he grasped her arm and held her back. Below them, in Harriet's room, a sound of voices had suddenly stopped, then there was the sound of rapid movement, of footsteps too heavy for Harriet's, of an opening door.

A man's voice called, " Who's there? "

Ginny answered, " It's me, Joe."

" Who's with you? "

" Colin."

There was a slight pause, then Joe said, " All right, come on in."

They went down the stairs to the basement.

Harriet was sitting by the electric fire. She looked very much as she had when Colin had seen her last, except that she was not actually crying. But her face had the blotchy look and the swollen eyelids that come from shedding so many tears that the marks of them will not fade. She was wearing a shabby velvet housecoat and bedroom slippers.

She did not move when she saw them. Looking fretfully at Ginny, she said, " My car—have you brought it back? Coming in like that, taking it, not saying you weren't coming back . . ."

Joe went over to her and patted her shoulder. There had been a big change in him since Colin had seen him in the Black Swan only a few evenings ago. The smooth, rubbery skin of his face that had never held any lines had sagged into loose folds and hollows. There were reddish pouches under his eyes, which had lost their darting brightness and had become almost vacant.

"Never mind about the car, darling," he said. "We've got other things to think about."

"But I do mind," Harriet said. "How does she think I can manage without it?"

"I'm very sorry, Mrs. Winter," Colin said, "it's at Turnhouse at the minute. I left it there. It's my fault."

"I don't believe it," Harriet said. "I mean, I don't believe it's your fault. Ginny left it there on purpose."

"Sh—don't worry about it." Joe patted away at her shoulder. "We've got plenty of other worries. You don't happen to have seen my wife, do you, Mr. Lockie? That's one worry. What's become of her. Not that I care. Not really, except that it's a sort of habit you get into, thinking you ought to know where your wife is."

Ginny had come a little way into the room. She was looking round it, taking note of it, as if it were a place that she wanted to be sure she would not forget, since she was not likely to come back to it.

She said wearily, "There's no need to go on pretending, Joe."

"Who's pretending what, darling?" he asked.

"Aren't you?" Ginny said. "Don't you know Beryl's in Scotland, still after that wretched picture? Don't you know it's supposed to be a Rubens? Don't you know that Willie Foster-Smith is dead and—and all the rest of it?"

"No, he doesn't!" Harriet cried. She came unsteadily to her feet, then sank back again in her chair. "He didn't know a damned thing till I went round on Monday evening and accused him and Beryl of fixing everything up between them. And if you'd stayed and listened to me instead of rushing off with my car, I could have told you so then."

"That's the truth," Joe said. "Well, not quite the truth." He sat down at the table, clasping his bald head in his hands. "God, my head's splitting in two! It's being pulled apart by red-hot pincers. What was I saying? . . . No, not quite the truth. Not quite."

"You mean you did know about the picture?" Ginny demanded.

"I had my suspicions, darling," he answered. "But that's not the same as knowing. Don't think it is. You can shut your eyes to suspicions for a hell of a long time. If Harriet hadn't come bursting in like she did, saying we'd murdered that chap Foster-Smith, and if I hadn't heard with my own ears what Beryl said back to her . . ." He gave a convulsive shudder. "Well, your wife's your wife. We were partners too. We ran the show together, giving people a fair deal—fair enough, anyway—that's what I thought. So I've gone on shutting my eyes as long as I could."

Ginny's eyes had remained on her mother while he was speaking. There was growing horror in them.

"Then you *did* know all about it. You *were* in on it . . . No, I don't believe it!" She dropped on her knees beside Harriet and threw her arms round her. "I don't believe it!"

Dazedly, Harriet held her, then as if she were half-afraid to make the gesture, began to pass her hand gently over Ginny's hair.

"I wasn't in on it, but it's all my fault, all the same," she said, her eyes starting to leak tears again. "I talked to Joe and Beryl, I showed them some of Willie's letters, the ones where he said he thought he was going to be able to prove that picture was a Rubens. Yet he'd *told* me not to say anything. He *told* me he wasn't saying anything to the

Lockies himself in case he was wrong and they had an awful disappointment."

She pulled several sodden handkerchiefs out of the pocket of her housecoat, chose the driest and dabbed with it at her eyes.

"And Beryl was much too interested," she said. " I ought to have noticed it. She didn't usually listen much when I talked. I ought to have noticed too she got much friendlier after that and started coming to see me and asking what news I'd had from my friend in Edinburgh. So when Willie wrote he'd persuaded the Lockies to let him have the picture for cleaning and that Colin was bringing it in to some firm that did that sort of thing, I told her all about it. I'm sorry, Colin." She looked at him over Ginny's head. "When Willie wrote about the theft, I thought it was a damned shame for your aunts, losing something valuable like that, but I never thought of Beryl having anything to do with it. And I thought Willie was right when he said he wasn't going to tell your aunts what he thought the picture was, because no one would believe him, and anyway, it would only make them feel worse about losing it."

"But why didn't you at least tell me about it?" Ginny asked. "You only said once that that old picture I used to be so fond of had been stolen with Colin's car."

"Well, darling, you were in one of your superior, stand-offish moods," Harriet said, "and I thought I'd pay you out by not telling you something you'd have loved to know. And then I simply forgot all about it. I don't suppose I gave it another thought till I got back from Spain and found Colin here and everyone steamed up about the sale. I was slow catching on even then."

"So was I, so was I ! " Joe gave a groan, kneading his burning temples.

" And when I began to catch on, I got scared," Harriet said.

Joe went on, " After you and Ginny came to see us, Mr. Lockie, I began to think at last . . . There was the idea of the picture popping up in our saleroom, of all places, after all we'd heard about it, and the way it popped up the moment Harriet went on holiday, Harriet being the one person, they thought, who just might recognise it. They never thought of Ginny having those tea-parties with the thing and so on, and that a kid's memory's often much clearer than a grown-up's. And then there was the whole market overt business. I tell you, it was hell when I began to think of those things. So I kept my eyes shut till Harriet came bursting in on Monday, saying we'd stolen the picture and murdered her Willie. And Beryl said . . ." His voice dried up.

Harriet took the story up quickly. " You see, I rang Willie up on Monday to tell him all the queer things that had been happening and ask his advice, and I heard he'd been killed. And it all seemed to make sense all of a sudden and I rushed round and—and Beryl said if I didn't keep my mouth shut, she'd show the police Willie's letters to me. I never even knew she had them. She stole them some time or other, just to be able to hold them over my head. And I was frightened. And then she went for me. She's small, but she's much stronger than me—that frightened me too. I'm an awful coward. I just grovelled and cried and begged her to stop. And she said that was only a taste of what would happen if Greer ever heard I suspected anything."

Colin went a few steps towards the table where Joe sat.

" You let that happen? " he asked. " I shouldn't have thought you'd stand by without interfering while your wife was beating up Mrs. Winter."

Joe raised his head slowly. His eyes darted to Harriet, then looked up at Colin. They were full of bewilderment and pain.

"Yes, I—of course I interfered," he muttered.

"But Joe, you're mixed up—that was all after you left," Harriet said.

Colin had known it was coming. Half-consciously he had been leading up to it, not sure in what form knowledge would come, or realising what deadly oppression there would be in the sudden weight of it.

"I was afraid of that," he said unwillingly. "I suppose the shock of having your eyes opened like that was just too much. You drove over to Hopewood, didn't you, to settle with Greer straight away? After all, he'd destroyed what you valued most in life, your integrity, your self-respect . . ."

Joe had begun to shake. Almost shrieking, he cried, "I didn't mean to. I only took the gun to protect myself. I never meant to kill anybody. But I couldn't stand it. Having been such a fool—so blind—just used by them!"

In a horrified voice, Harriet exclaimed, "Joe, think what you're saying!"

Another voice spoke from the doorway. "It's a bit late for that. He should have done his thinking a long time ago."

With a gun in his gloved hand, Herbert Stringer came into the room.

He moved quite silently in rubber-soled shoes. He was wearing a felt hat pulled down low over his white hair and only just showing his eyebrows. They were dark again, as they had been when Colin had first seen him lying in the road near Ardachoil and as they had always been when he saw them in nightmares.

"You all heard him," Stringer said. "You know it was him killed Greer. It wasn't me. Now he's going to write that down and sign it." His hand moved swiftly so that the gun pointed at Colin. "No, Mr. Lockie, you stay where you are. You don't want to get hurt, do you?"

"What good is this going to do you?" Colin asked.

"You leave that to me."

"You'll get life for the other things you've done." Colin did not know why he felt that he had to keep on talking, unless it was to give Joe a chance to get hold of himself, to stop that helpless shaking.

"What else *have* I done?" Stringer asked with a mocking light in the eyes under the dark eyebrows. "Anything you can prove. My friend, Mr. Greer, was a very law-abiding gentleman, never been in trouble in his life, and I looked after him, that's all."

"What about the things you stole from his house after he was killed?" Colin asked.

"I never stole anything. You ask Joe here who took them."

"It's a lie," Joe said violently. The accusation seemed to steady him. "I never took a thing."

"Not when you and Beryl came back to fix things to look as if I'd done it?"

"You know we didn't."

"Didn't come back?"

"Didn't——" Joe's voice faltered. "Didn't take anything. You were filling your pockets before I left the house. That was all you could think of, to take what you could and get away."

"With Greer's body inside, in his study, where it could have stayed for a week or two without anyone knowing anything about it. How did it get out on the steps, if you didn't come back and put it there?"

"All right, I went back," Joe said. "Beryl said it was the thing to do. She said the body had to be found quickly, when they could still tell how long ago he died, and if anyone had heard the shots, they'd still remember just when they heard them. Because she'd an alibi for that time. She was in the saleroom all the evening, where lots of people were sure to have seen her. And she said she could say I'd been there too and people wouldn't remember they'd never actually seen me till later."

"That wasn't your only reason," Stringer said with an ugly twist of his mouth. "You wanted the police to get after me."

Colin said, "You're wrong, you know. If that's how it happened, Mrs. Lake was hoping the police would get after Miss Winter and me."

Stringer turned on him furiously. "You keep out of this! You've made enough trouble already."

"Joe," Ginny said. Still on the floor beside Harriet, she had sat back on her heels and was holding Harriet firmly by the wrist, keeping her still. "Joe, were you there when I came?"

"That's right, Ginny," he answered miserably. "I'd just done it and this chap rushed in and—and there we were—and then I heard you calling. So I kept the gun on him till you'd gone. That's something I'm glad of anyway. I don't know what he'd have done if I hadn't."

"Who, me? I wouldn't have done a thing, Miss Winter," Stringer said. "I'm not a violent man. I'm quiet and law-abiding. If you want to know what I did when I found the body of my employer, I blacked out and went wandering off in a state of shock. And I can't remember a thing till I found myself in the old Sibbald house this evening. Can't think why I went there except that I knew it was empty."

"And that you happened to have the key," Colin said.

Stringer gave a slight shrug of his shoulders. "Who knows? I can't remember. But as soon as my memory came back, I came out and I bought a newspaper and then I saw the body'd been found on the steps and they were looking for me. And that's not right, I thought. Apart from the fact I didn't kill him, there's the matter of Mr. Greer's will. He was very generous to me in his will, that I know. Left me the contents of his house and *that*——" He swung round on Colin. "That includes the picture there's been all the palaver about. That picture was legally his, bought in the open market. So now it's mine and you needn't think I'll be afraid to fight to get it back. Not when I've got Joe's confession, I won't! So that's what I've come for. I want it just the way I heard it when I was listening at the door. How did it go? 'I didn't mean to—I couldn't stand it—having been so blind——'"

"All right," Joe said. "It's best, I dare say. I'll write it." He looked round vaguely. "Where's some paper."

"Have you got some paper and a pen, Mrs. Winter?" Stringer asked.

Harriet gave a convulsive jerk at hearing her own name, but her face was blank.

Ginny said in a low voice, "Over there in the bureau."

"All right, you get it, Miss Winter," Stringer said.

She got up and went to the bureau. As she opened it, he went on, "Don't try any tricks. I can pull this trigger much faster than you can do anything."

She took out a block of paper and a ball-point pen.

"Now give them to Joe," Stringer said, "then get back to where you were."

Ginny put the block and the pen on the table in front of Joe, then went back to stand beside Harriet.

"Get writing, Joe," Stringer said. "Go on. You can start, 'I never meant to kill anyone . . .'"

Joe's fingers fumbled for the pen, picked it up, dropped it, picked it up again.

"I won't say I stole those things," he said in a thick voice, as if he were talking in his sleep. "I'll confess to the murder. I won't say I stole."

"All right, it won't make any difference," Stringer said. "They'll find the things in your house and draw their own conclusions."

"I didn't steal," Joe said. "That's how I'll begin. I'll say, 'I have never in my life stooped——'"

There was a wild scream from Harriet. "Don't, don't, don't, Joe! Don't you see, when you've done it, he'll kill us all and say you did it?"

For an instant Stringer was startled. His hand wavered. At the same moment Colin and Joe hurled themselves across the room at him. The noise of the gun was shatteringly loud in the room and one other scream was added to those that poured uncontrollably from Harriet's stretched throat.

Then Joe began to topple to the ground. It seemed to happen very slowly. His face was empty and blood was spurting over his shirt and his cream satin tie with the hounds racing up it and his tartan waistcoat. But Stringer was on the ground too, with Colin on top of him. This time Stringer was unconscious as Colin had only thought he was at the first meeting.

Ginny had pulled the window open and was shouting for help. In a moment feet came pounding along the pavements and the sleeping square came to life, a crowd mysteriously materialising where there had been only the bare cobbles of the cold market place, as a crowd always can, even out of silence and darkness.

CHAPTER FIFTEEN

IT WAS BY CHANCE, some months later, that a paragraph in *The Scotsman* which stated that the appeal of Herbert Stringer against his conviction for the murder of Joseph Lake had been dismissed, was in the same issue as one announcing that a portrait of Lady Arabella Hamilton, believed to be by Peter Paul Rubens, would be in a sale of pictures to be held at Sotheby's next day.

Since Joe's murder and the trial of Herbert Stringer had occurred in the far South, half a dozen lines disposed of the matter. The sale of the portrait was dealt with at far greater length. Its owners, after all, came of an old Edinburgh family and were resident in Scotland. The picture, besides, had first been identified as a Rubens by the late William Foster-Smith, whose books on the artistic treasures of Scotland had gained him, *The Scotsman* considered, a well-merited reputation.

On the Women's Page there were photographs of the three Lockie sisters and some of their remarks on what it had felt like to find themselves owners of a painting by Rubens.

"I sometimes wish we'd never found out," the eldest Miss Lockie was quoted as saying.

"We were so fond of her as she was before," said Miss Phyllis Lockie.

"And now we have to get rid of her, in case we have burglars," said Miss Dorothy Lockie.

"But of course we do not despise the money," said all three together.

A strange and romantic part of the story, the writer continued, was that the painting had actually been stolen once already, when it was being sent for cleaning to Edinburgh, by thieves who had had no idea of its value, but had only wanted the car for a getaway. Then more than two years after the theft, it had been recognised in a saleroom by an old friend of the Lockies', who had bought it and returned it to them. And romance had followed romance, for the friend, Miss Virginia Winter, had recently become engaged to be married to Dr. Colin Lockie, in whose car the painting had been when it was stolen.

Colin was shown this story by a colleague in the University Staff Club, who asked, as Colin handed the paper back, "Isn't it embarrassing to read that sort of thing about yourself?"

"Believe me, it could have been far worse," Colin answered and proceeded to the bar, where Virginia, as he had been slowly getting into the habit of calling her, was to pick him up and tell him how she had fared during an afternoon of house-hunting.

Indeed, he thought, it could have been far, far worse.

Stringer's defence at his trial had been that on seeing his employer killed by the lunatic, Lake, he had had a black-out and could remember nothing until he had come to himself in a strange, empty house. Why he had gone there, he had no idea, but on recovering his memory, he had immediately tried to track down the murderer, who, on being charged with his guilt, had attacked him, so that Stringer had had to shoot him in self-defence.

Counsel for the defence had claimed that Joe Lake had certainly been insane, since he had apparently believed that his wife had been carrying on a love affair with Edmund Greer, of which there was no evidence at all. There was no evidence that she had even met Mr. Greer, except most briefly in the saleroom, where he had occasionally bid for some articles that had taken his fancy—a Sheraton tea-caddy, for instance, and a Queen Anne

soup ladle. It remained a bit of a mystery, of course, what
had happened to Mrs. Lake. Nothing had been seen or
heard of her since the day following Greer's murder, except
for the rumour that she had been seen in Scotland. A
woman answering to her description was said to have been
chased out of their home, late one night, by three elderly
ladies, armed with golf-clubs. But wasn't there a certain
improbability about that story?

Without anything actually having been said on the
matter, a feeling had begun to go round the court that if
Beryl Lake turned up again, it would be as a corpse, done
to death by her husband.

However, the jury had not liked the look of Stringer.
The story that they had chosen to believe was that the
accused, on finding Greer dead, had assumed at once that
he would be suspected, had promptly helped himself to
what he could in the house and gone into hiding. But later
he had had second thoughts. He had realised that his
actions had made it impossible for him to claim any legacy
his employer might have left him, so he had set out to
obtain a signed confession from Joe Lake, and had been
meaning, as soon as he had it, to shoot Lake in cold blood,
together with the three other people in the room, to leave
the gun in Joe's hand and disappear once more, later to
be found wandering with his memory still missing.

Somehow, all through the trial, all mention of the picture
had been avoided. Colin and Ginny had had to give
evidence and for a few days their names had occurred
uncomfortably often in the Press, yet they had been asked
no questions about their trip to Hopewood on the night of
the murder. Before the trial, of course, there had been
endless sessions with the police, during which both of them
had made and signed long statements which gave a full
account of their actions. But neither prosecution nor defence
had thought that it would help either case to bemuse the

jury with the complexities of market overt, so a curtain
had been allowed to fall over the adventures of the Decayed
Gentlewoman. Colin was sure that in fact the police had
never believed a word of it.

He had ordered drinks for himself and Ginny and they
had just been put down in front of him when he saw her
coming towards him. She was carrying a newspaper and he
noticed that she had a slightly flushed look of excitement.
Thinking that she must have been reading the interview
with the aunts, or else seen the note about Stringer, he
picked up the drinks and went to meet her. He was
preparing to tell her that this must be pretty well the last
that they would hear of Stringer and that it was time to
start thinking of other things, for reminders of the time
in Oldersfield had unpredictable effects on her spirits. She
and Harriet had both grieved for Joe, Harriet so much that
she had sold the café and had gone off to try to forget her
sorrows on a bus-tour in Yugoslavia.

But Colin's concern was unnecessary. With her usual
single-mindedness, Ginny, on the trail of a flat, had not
thought of reading anything in the newspapers but the property advertisements, and her excitement was because she
had seen and fallen in love with a flat.

" It's really a beauty," she said as they sat down together.
" It's extraordinary to find anything like it on my first day
out hunting. But it's been an altogether extraordinary day.
I thought I knew Scotland pretty well, but it turns out I'm
a complete foreigner. These advertisements are written
in a language I've never even heard spoken before. Of
course I know everyone's a foreigner when it comes to
reading house-agents' prose, but listen—what's a main
door house? What's a lower flatted villa? What's a public
roup? Well, never mind, I've found this wonderful flat
and I've got the keys here and I thought we might go
round now to take a look at it together. Then, if you like

it, I thought we might write this evening, making an offer——"

"Not on your life!" Colin broke in, making her turn a startled face to him.

"But it's really wonderful, Colin," she said. "It's true the bathroom's just an old cupboard and hasn't got a window, and the kitchen's a very forbidding sort of place, and I've no idea how we'd warm it, but still, it's got lovely big Georgian rooms with exquisite ceilings and one Adam fireplace, which I'm almost ready to believe is a real one, and——"

"That isn't the point." Firmly Colin stemmed the flow. "In Scotland, if you make an offer in a letter and it's accepted by letter, that's a sale. You don't have to wait for a contract to be signed. You don't put down a deposit. It's complete, finished."

"I see," she said. "That sounds nice and quick and easy."

"Yes, but try writing that letter yourself and you're probably going to find yourself stuck with the place, with no chance to back out, even if it's crumbling with dry rot. So it's very important to get it written by a lawyer, who knows how to put in all the necessary conditions on which we make the offer."

"Ah, a lawyer." He saw a gleam in her eyes. "So here we go again. I wonder what strange things he'll have to tell us this time. I'll tell you something, Colin—going to lawyers could easily become a vice with me. They tell you such amazing, improbable things. No one else would ever dare tell you such improbable things. It's very stimulating to the imagination."

MORE TITLES AVAILABLE FROM
CORONET CRIME

ELIZABETH FERRARS

☐	53029 4	Alive and Dead	£3.50
☐	51590 2	A Foot in the Grave	£2.99
☐	43053 2	Murder Among Friends	£2.50

LINDA BARNES

☐	53538 5	The Snake Tattoo	£3.50
☐	50919 8	A Trouble of Fools	£3.50

MARGERY ALLINGHAM

☐	53540 7	The Return of Mr Campion	£2.99

BETTY ROWLANDS

☐	54415 5	A Little Gentle Sleuthing	£3.99

All these books are available at your local bookshop or newsagent, or can be ordered direct from the publisher. Just tick the titles you want and fill in the form below.

Prices and availability subject to change without notice.

Hodder & Stoughton Paperbacks, P.O. Box 11, Falmouth, Cornwall.

Please send cheque or postal order, and allow the following for postage and packing:

U.K. – 80p for one book and 20p for each additional book ordered up to a £2.00 maximum.

B.F.P.O. – 80p for the first book, plus 20p for each additional book

OVERSEAS INCLUDING EIRE – £1.50 for the first book, plus £1.00 for the second book, and 30p for each additional book ordered.

OR Please debit this amount from my Access/Visa Card (delete as appropriate).

Card Number ⌊ ⌊ ⌊ ⌊ ⌊ ⌊ ⌊ ⌊ ⌊ ⌊ ⌊ ⌊ ⌊ ⌊ ⌊ ⌊ ⌋

Name ....

Address ....

....